Please Me

Also from J. Kenner

The Stark Trilogy:
Release Me
Claim Me
Complete Me
Anchor Me
Lost With Me, Coming Oct. 2018

Stark Ever After:
Take Me
Have Me
Play My Game
Seduce Me
Unwrap Me
Deepest Kiss
Entice Me
Hold Me
Please Me
Damien, Coming Jan. 2019

Stark International
Steele Trilogy:
Say My Name
On My Knees
Under My Skin
Take My Dare (novella, includes bonus short story: Steal My Heart)

Stark World Standalone Stories:
Justify Me (part of the Lexi Blake Crossover Collection)
One Night (short story)

Jamie & Ryan Novellas:
Tame Me
Tempt Me

Please Me

A Stark Ever After Novella

By J. Kenner

1001 Dark Nights

EVIL EYE

CONCEPTS

Please Me
A Stark Ever After Novella
By J. Kenner

Copyright 2018 Julie Kenner
ISBN: 978-1-948050-17-3

Published by Evil Eye Concepts, Incorporated

This is a work of fiction. Names, places, characters and incidents are the product of the author's imagination and are fictitious. Any resemblance to actual persons, living or dead, events or establishments is solely coincidental.

Sign up for the 1001 Dark Nights Newsletter
and be entered to win a Tiffany Key necklace.

There's a contest every month!

Go to www.1001DarkNights.com to subscribe.

As a bonus, all subscribers will receive a free copy of
Discovery Bundle Three
Featuring stories by
Sidney Bristol, Darcy Burke, T. Gephart
Stacey Kennedy, Adriana Locke
JB Salsbury, and Erika Wilde

One Thousand and One Dark Nights

Once upon a time, in the future...

*I was a student fascinated with stories and learning.
I studied philosophy, poetry, history, the occult, and
the art and science of love and magic. I had a vast
library at my father's home and collected thousands
of volumes of fantastic tales.*

*I learned all about ancient races and bygone
times. About myths and legends and dreams of all
people through the millennium. And the more I read
the stronger my imagination grew until I discovered
that I was able to travel into the stories... to actually
become part of them.*

*I wish I could say that I listened to my teacher
and respected my gift, as I ought to have. If I had, I
would not be telling you this tale now.
But I was foolhardy and confused, showing off
with bravery.*

*One afternoon, curious about the myth of the
Arabian Nights, I traveled back to ancient Persia to
see for myself if it was true that every day Shahryar
(Persian: شهریار, "king") married a new virgin, and then
sent yesterday's wife to be beheaded. It was written
and I had read, that by the time he met Scheherazade,
the vizier's daughter, he'd killed one thousand
women.*

Something went wrong with my efforts. I arrived in the midst of the story and somehow exchanged places with Scheherazade — a phenomena that had never occurred before and that still to this day, I cannot explain.

Now I am trapped in that ancient past. I have taken on Scheherazade's life and the only way I can protect myself and stay alive is to do what she did to protect herself and stay alive.

Every night the King calls for me and listens as I spin tales. And when the evening ends and dawn breaks, I stop at a point that leaves him breathless and yearning for more. And so the King spares my life for one more day, so that he might hear the rest of my dark tale.

As soon as I finish a story... I begin a new one... like the one that you, dear reader, have before you now.

Chapter One

"Well, I think it's a brilliant idea," I say, squatting on the floor and smiling into my daughter's eyes, even though the words are meant for Abby, my business partner. "And so does Anne, don't you, my sweet little girl?"

"Mama!" She belts the word, and it wraps around me like a hug to my heart. Her chubby arms reach for me as she toddles over, and I eagerly cuddle her close as she yawns and rubs her eyes, then snuggles against me. It's forty minutes past her usual nap time, and although she's peaceful now, I know that crankiness is imminent if I don't get her down pronto.

Carefully, I settle her into the white crib that takes up a large chunk of the space beside my desk. "Nap time," I say, then bend over and give her forehead a kiss. "Time for Anne to go sleepy-bye and dream of Miss Abby's awesome idea."

As her lids flutter closed, she reaches for me. But I know it's not Mommy she wants but her blankie, and I bend down to grab the striped hospital blanket that came home with us just shy of twenty months ago. We've tried urging stuffed animals on her. A smiling tiger. A silly giraffe. But no animal wins out over her blankie.

Her lips curve into a smile at the same time as her little fingers curl around the blanket. I feel a hitch in my chest, as if the weight of my love for this tiny little person is too much to bear. Then I draw in a breath and try to shift my thoughts away from my youngest daughter and back to the world of smartphone apps.

When I turn, Abby flashes a wide grin, her eyes shining with humor. "You're cracking me up, Nikki," she whispers. "I mean, this has got to be the weirdest developmental meeting ever."

I lift a shoulder in a casual shrug. "What can I say?" I whisper back. "I like to be different." I grab the baby monitor, then nod toward the back door and the patio beyond where we can talk without the risk of waking my little girl. "Come on."

Anne's always been a good sleeper. But like her namesake, Ashley Anne Fairchild Price, she's a cranky little monster if she doesn't get enough.

My sister Ashley was my rock when I was growing up, the reason I survived the horror of a childhood with our mother at the helm. I relied on Ashley. Looked up to her. And loved her unconditionally.

But dear God, that girl was a bitch if she didn't get a good night's sleep.

My youngest, I fear, is going to be a lot like her auntie.

The thought makes my chest tighten again, only this time the love is tainted with pain. Because Anne will never know my sister. For so many years, I'd believed that Ashley had escaped from the hell our mother had inflicted on us. I thought that only I remained caught in her spiderweb, forced to starve and suffer all sorts of abuse at my mother's hand simply so that I could be her pretty, polished pageant doll.

Cutting had been my ultimate escape. A release valve for all the horror and pain that built up inside of me. And when the deep cuts on my thighs rendered me useless in a bathing suit competition, I finally found my freedom. From that particular horror, anyway.

Ashley's escape was more permanent. Believing that she'd failed as a wife—that she would never live up to that model of perfection our mother so rigidly demanded—she killed herself.

Her death ripped a hole in my heart.

I've missed her for years, but now that I have children, her absence weighs on me even more. Now there are two little girls who will never know their aunt. And I'm the only one who will ever truly understand the hole Ashley's absence will leave in their lives.

"You okay?" Abby catches my eye before settling into one of the upholstered patio chairs.

"Fine," I say, then manufacture a smile, willing my mood to match the lie. "Mind wandering." I take the chair next to her so that we're both looking out over the pristine Malibu beach and the crashing waves of the Pacific beyond.

We're at the beachfront cottage Damien built for me before we had kids. I'd mentioned that the only thing our stunning hillside house lacked was a back door that opened right onto the sand.

Because he spoils me rotten, Damien surprised me with the bungalow. It's at the base of our property, accessed by a winding path that leads to the main house. It's small but beautifully designed. And when I learned about the cottage, a wild mixture of awe and joy fluttered through me.

Awe from the fact that Damien could so cavalierly decide to build a house. Joy from the reality that he did it for no purpose other than because it would make me happy.

I come from Texas oil and gas money, so I'm no stranger to the finer things in life. But compared to Damien, I grew up in abject poverty. Not that he always had his billions. No, Damien Stark fought for the life he's built and for everything he's ever owned. And that, I think with a small smile, includes me.

I'm still not sure what lucky star shined down and blessed me with Damien's love, but I know that it is real and unfathomably deep. I know, because he tells me so. More important, he shows me. In every touch, every kiss, every silly or extravagant gift. He is my heart and my soul. My breath and my body.

And the miracle is that I love him just as completely.

We know each other, he and I. Intimately. Passionately. Fully and completely.

Which is why I'm absolutely certain that something is troubling him. Something he hasn't told me about, but that's been bothering him for a couple of days. And though I tell myself that it must be trouble at work—because between the two of us he's promised me no more secrets—somehow I don't quite believe it.

Beside me, Abby leans back with a sigh, and I force my thoughts back to the present, reluctantly letting go of my fears and worries.

"You know," Abby says thoughtfully, "I thought our offices in Studio City were nice. But this is definitely a step up." She shifts to face me directly. "Can we have wine?"

I laugh. "Why, Abigail Jones, I'm shocked."

She rolls her eyes. "No, you're not. Besides, you're the one who keeps saying how awesome the new app idea is. We need to toast it."

"Can't argue with that." And since I try to be accommodating to my guests and business partners—and since a glass of Chardonnay sounds great—I grab a bottle from the small outdoor wine fridge, then pour a glass for each of us.

"To you," I say. "And to the Mommy Watch app."

The temporary name sucks—we both know that—but the idea is great. Abby's come up with an idea for a smartphone app designed specifically for new moms who've returned to the workplace. It will integrate all the various mommy resources that are already out there in one place. Video or audio baby monitoring, nanny cams, Q&A resources, growth logs, mommy's weight loss logs, and a zillion other options, ultimately providing a new mom with a unified mommy's helper app.

I figure it's a winner. And since Abby's a whiz at coding—which is why I hired her in the first place—I know she can pull it off.

"And you really don't think we should wait on it?" she asks.

"I really don't." I mean what I say, but I do understand her hesitation. Not much more than a year ago, Abby had been my employee, and I was a frustrated wreck trying to be a mom and a business owner.

With Damien's resources, of course, I didn't have to work at all, and I knew it. But the whole reason I'd come to LA from Dallas was to start my own development company. The fact that I married a master of the universe didn't change any of that.

My girls, however, did. Our almost four-year-old, Lara, was twenty months old when we adopted her, and I got pregnant with Anne right before we left for China. I'd intended to go back to work full time after three months with the girls and working from the kitchen table.

All that had changed when I'd stepped foot in the office. I'd realized, painfully, that I wanted to be home for Anne's first steps and her first words. I wanted to watch my oldest, Lara, play with our cat or bang out a tune on the piano. I wanted to laugh as she watched *Dora the Explorer* and sang the map song. And, dammit, I wanted to go to Gymboree with her and bounce balls in a nylon parachute.

But I wanted my career, too.

So after much soul-searching, I compromised. I offered Abby a partnership. I closed our Studio City office, saving myself hours on the road. And I converted my beloved bungalow into an office.

Now our receptionist/office manager, Marge, comes here three days a week. Abby works from home or comes to the bungalow when we need a meeting. And though my original plan had been to keep the business stumbling along servicing existing clients and projects, things have been going so well that we recently took on two additional clients and one new employee.

And, of course, we're getting back into developing original content. Like Abby's app.

"Yes," I say, returning to the topic with a decisive nod. "Absolutely, we should move forward. You can get Travis on it with you."

She nods thoughtfully, her attention firmly on the ocean. "He'd be good."

I bite back a smile. Travis joined Fairchild Development as a programmer two months ago, and he and Abby hit it off immediately. She's totally unwilling to admit the same to me—probably because she's afraid I'll disapprove. But so long as the sparks between them don't impact the work, I haven't got a problem.

"Anything else that we haven't gone over?"

Abby flips through the black leather portfolio with *Fairchild & Partners Development* monogrammed on the front. She scribbles a few notes, scratches through a few lines, then turns to me with a shrug. "I think we've hit everything. So I'll talk to Travis in the morning? I can meet him for breakfast near my place, or we could meet here."

I shake my head. "I'm taking tomorrow off. Remember? Long weekend."

She lifts her glass to me. "The upside of being the boss. Have a good day off."

I think of my elaborate plans for the weekend. Plans that involve Damien, candlelight, and a significant amount of time in bed. A warm flush spreads over my skin, and I raise my glass in return. "Believe me," I say with conviction. "I intend to."

Chapter Two

By the time Anne wakes up, Abby and I have each downed two glasses of wine, and I insist that she leave her car and let Edward take her home.

"Oh, I don't want to—"

"It's no trouble. It's his job. And I promise you he enjoys it. Besides, he only listens to his audiobooks when he's on the road, and I happen to know that he's almost to the end of the latest Steve Berry thriller. Trust me when I say he wants to go for a drive."

She laughs but agrees, and I shoot Edward a text asking him to pull the limo around and meet us in the circular drive that fronts the house.

Abby raises a brow. "A limo?"

I shrug. "What's the fun of having a limo at my disposal if I can't send my partner home in it?"

"Eric blew it big time," she says, referring to the second of my former business development execs. He took a job in New York only a few days before my decision to cut back—and to make Abby a partner.

"He's having the time of his life in Manhattan," I say. Which is probably true. But the more relevant truth is that I miss having him on my team. Abby and I excel on the tech side. But Eric was a whiz at client relations. He thrived on wining and dining potential and existing clients. Me, I'd rather hunker down with my keyboard.

To be honest, I've been following his career. And while he's doing well, he's not standing out. The company that he went to work for was bought out. Now Eric's a small fish in a big pond. And I can't help but wonder if he'd like to come back to being a big fish in a smaller pond.

That, however, is a problem for another day. Right now, I just want to get back to the house. Back to Damien and the kids.

As soon as I've changed Anne, we head up the crushed stone path that leads to the main house, my little girl toddling alongside me, holding my hand. Abby gives a low, appreciative whistle when she sees the limo, not to mention Edward, who is decked out in his uniform, perfectly pressed and starched. "Madam," he says, opening the door for her. As he does, I see that he's stocked the bar, and I give him an appreciative nod. He doesn't respond—he's far too professional—but I see the glint of amusement in his eyes.

"North Hollywood," he says, indicating the text I sent earlier. "Should be plenty of time to finish my book."

"You're welcome," I say with a laugh, and this time I earn myself a full-blown smile. "Feel free to take the evening off," I add, knowing that Damien drove his new Tesla to the office this morning. "But we'll see you at ten tomorrow?" He's in charge of morning transportation for my surprise for Damien.

"Of course, Mrs. Stark."

I've repeatedly told him to call me Nikki, and he's repeatedly ignored me. At this point, I think I need to give up and declare Edward the winner.

I watch as they pull out of the drive, waving at the tinted window behind which Abby sits, presumably either waving back or pouring herself another drink. I remember the first time I was chauffeured in that limo, and a hot flood of sensual awareness courses through me, the memory making my body hum. I close my eyes, reveling in the heat and the memory of Damien's voice surrounding me. Teasing me. Commanding me.

I did things that night I would never have imagined doing, submitting totally to Damien's firm voice and sensual commands. I still do. The connection between us is so strong it's like a physical bond, which is why I'm so troubled by the fact that he's been distracted and distant these last few days, but hasn't told me why.

I sigh and call to Anne, who's wandered off to look at rocks. She hurries over, and I take her hand, preparing to head inside. But I stop when I hear the sharp beep of a horn underscored by the rumble of an engine. An instant later, a sleek, classic Thunderbird convertible careens into view, then screeches to a halt in the spot previously occupied by the limo.

"Ryan actually let you drive that?" I ask my best friend, Jamie, as she pulls off her scarf in true Grace Kelly fashion. It's a fitting comparison. Jamie might be dark instead of blonde, but like the princess, she's got a stunning, unique style that the camera absolutely adores. I'm photogenic and pretty, but my looks are of the wholesome, blonde, girl-next-door variety. Whereas Jamie is the epitome of sophistication, elegance, and sensuality.

Jamie tilts her head up in response to my question. "This old thing? He has a new toy now. Honestly, we should never let them shop together."

Damien and Ryan both now own the latest Teslas, not yet available to the general public. But I don't believe her about it being open season in the Hunter family garage. Ryan babies that Thunderbird—and he knows damn well that Jamie isn't the most careful driver on the planet.

"You snagged the keys the second he left for London this morning, didn't you?"

She bats her eyes innocently. "He left them in the back of his desk drawer, behind the box of stamps. That's practically an engraved invitation."

I refrain from responding. I need to set a good example for Anne, after all.

Jamie falls in step beside me, then puts down her hand for Anne to grab. "Hey, there, cutie. Did you miss your Aunt Jamie?"

Jamie's not actually related to me, but we've been best friends forever, and we're definitely family.

"We're going to have such fun this weekend," she tells Anne, who jumps up and down, clearly excited to see Jamie.

"Big plans?" I ask.

"We're going to have a girls' weekend, aren't we, Princess?"

"Pinciss!" Anne repeats, and Jamie winks at me.

"See?" she says. "We're going to have a blast."

"Just don't corrupt my kids, okay?"

Damien doesn't know it yet, but I'm whisking him away for a romantic weekend. And since that's pretty much impossible with two little girls in tow, Jamie volunteered to babysit. To say I'm grateful would be an understatement, because about an hour after I'd finalized all my arrangements, our live-in nanny, Bree, asked if she could take a long weekend to go to Vegas for her sister's unannounced, elopement-style wedding.

Fortunately, Jamie's husband is in Europe through next week checking in with all of the heads of security for the various European divisions of Stark International. Jamie didn't go with him because she was supposed to work, but when her schedule freed up, she volunteered to babysit in what was either a legitimate moment of female solidarity or a complete and total shift into insanity.

I'm going with solidarity.

Whatever her reason, I'm grateful. And even though Jamie can be a spazz, I also know that she'll watch my kids like a hawk and guard them with her life. Best of all, Jamie agreed to stay in the house, which is decked out with top-of-the-line security, baby monitors galore, and a well-stocked kitchen and wet bar. The latter being more for Jamie than for the kids. Plus, Jamie knows the place well. She's stayed in our guest house a number of times, but of course that's Bree's place now. So this weekend, Jamie's staying in the first-floor guest suite, which isn't too shabby if I do say so myself.

As we open the front door, I'm almost bowled over by the high pitched "Mama!" that emanates from Lara's almost four-year-old lungs. She barrels toward me, her short legs pumping, then clings to my leg. "I missed you, Mama! I love you!"

I reach down and scoop her up. "I love you right back, baby girl. Did you have fun with Miss Bree today?"

"We painted," Bree said, smiling from where she'd halted at the base of the stairs.

"I thought maybe," I reply with a smile. My little girl's shoulder-length coal black hair is dappled with yellow at the tips, and there's a blob of green right on the end of her nose.

"It's water-based," Bree assures me. "It'll wash right out."

"Well, if it doesn't, that's fine. I think it's a fashion statement."

Bree laughs at the same time that Lara notices Jamie and releases my leg in favor of the prodigal aunt. As Jamie navigates both kids—I figure she might as well dive into the weekend now—I head over to Bree.

"When are you going?"

"Now, if that's okay. I've already packed my stuff into my car."

"That's fine," I assure her. "Drive safe and congratulate your sister for me."

"Will do. And I'll be back late on Sunday, so I can get the kids up on Monday morning. Do you need me to do anything for tomorrow before I go?" Bree had helped me make some of the arrangements for my surprise, but now I just shake my head.

"It's all under control."

"Sweet," she says, then grins mischievously. "Have a good time."

"That's my plan."

As soon as she's out the door, I turn my attention to the girls. "Daddy's home soon. Should we make snacks?"

"Teddy Grahams!" Lara squeals.

Jamie cocks her head. "I was hoping for the adult variety liquid snack."

"Gotcha covered. And as for you, little rugrat," I say as I scoop Lara up and hang her upside down, "I think apples and cheese for a little girl, and something a little more interesting for Daddy. Okay?"

She tries to bob her head, but since she's upside down, she just shimmies in my arms.

The house boasts a huge, commercial grade kitchen on the first floor, but I never use it. Instead, we climb the massive free-floating staircase to the third floor, then cross the open area to the smaller, normal-human sized kitchen that was originally intended as prep space for caterers.

It's still used for parties, but for the most part, the smaller kitchen has become the heart of our home, and as soon as I put Lara down, she scrambles to the breakfast table where her coloring books and crayons are scattered.

As she scribbles madly, Jamie pours wine, and I slice up fruit and cheese, then toss some crackers into a bowl. When

Damien arrives, I'll pull out olives and some chicken salad I picked up at the deli. Not wildly extravagant, but nice enough to accompany the bourbon I'm sure he'll want.

I've just popped a cube of Wisconsin Cheddar into my mouth when my phone chimes, signaling a call from Damien. "Hey," I say through a mouthful of cheese. "Are you in the car?"

"Actually, I'm stuck here. It's been one of those days."

"Oh." Disappointment crashes over me, along with the fear that my plans for a long weekend are going to be swept away in a flood of work crises. I draw in a breath and catch Jamie's eye, her expression sympathetic. "Well, Jamie's here. She can watch the kids, and I could come stay the night at the Tower Apartment." Stark International is based in Stark Tower, one of LA's downtown high rises. Damien's private office takes up half the top floor, and his—now our—private apartment takes up the other half of the space.

"That's tempting, but no. I need…"

As he trails off, that knot of worry in my stomach starts to tighten. "What?" I whisper, hoping that now, finally, he'll tell me what's the matter.

"I need to deal with this."

"Damien, please—"

"I'll be home as soon as I can. I promise. I love you. Kiss the girls for me. And I'll see you later tonight."

I hesitate, waiting to hear those familiar words: *Until then, imagine me, touching you.* But there's only silence, and I swallow rising tears. "I love you, too. Do you want to talk to La—" I begin, but he's already clicked off.

I draw a breath and stare at my phone before lifting my head and meeting Jamie's eyes.

"I'm sorry," she says. "But honestly, Nicholas, the man pretty much runs the entire known universe. Of course there's stuff on his mind."

She's right, and I draw in a breath, suck it up, and force myself into a good mood as we change into swimsuits, then take the kids onto the back patio. Lara's becoming a little fish, so I let her put on her floaties and splash in the shallow end as Jamie and I dangle our feet in the water, our wine now in plastic cups. We talk about everything and nothing, the way best friends do, as we watch my oldest giggle as she blows bubbles in the water and leaps fearlessly off the side of the pool. Behind us, Anne plays with a LEGO Duplo set quietly in the shaded activity pop-up, not yet ready to brave the pool.

All in all, it's a perfect day, marred only by my lingering fears that won't dissolve no matter how much I try and will them to.

Later, Jamie does the honor of reading to Lara. Her favorite is still *Good Night, Sleep Tight, Little Bunnies*, and both Damien and I have it memorized. As Jamie takes care of my oldest, I read *Goodnight, Gorilla* to Anne and then settle her into her crib. I linger, watching her sweet face as she drifts off to sleep, grateful that I have such easy kids. Not that there aren't tears and crankiness, but today was a tantrum-free day.

And hallelujah for that.

Jamie and I meet up again on the patio, and I keep my phone open to the monitoring app as we settle down for more snacking and chatting. I feel like a teenager at a slumber party again, although that illusion fades when Jamie yawns deeply, then stands up and announces that she's going to bed. Jamie *never* crashed when we were teens. She would have considered it a red mark of failure.

When I remind her of this, she just shrugs and shoots me an impish grin. "Yeah, but the reason I'm tired now is that last night Ryan and I fucked like bunnies, and I didn't get any sleep at all, what with all that goodbye sex."

"Right," I say dryly. "I should have known."

"Coming in?"

I take another sip of my wine and shake my head. "You go on. I'm going to stay out here and watch the stars a bit longer." I glance once again at my phone, just as I've been doing all evening, but there are no emails or texts from Damien.

"The longer he works, the less stressed he'll be about playing hooky tomorrow," Jamie says sagely.

I nod, knowing she's right but still wishing Damien was home with me.

"Night, Nicholas," she says.

"Night, James," I return, answering in kind with our childhood nicknames for each other.

She heads back inside for the guest suite, and I look up at the sky, smiling when I see a shooting star streak across the moonless night. Once again, I crave Damien beside me, but this time when I turn to my phone, I hear a rustling come over the speaker. The video component of the monitor isn't working—I'd meant to fix it today and forgot—but it doesn't matter. Either our cat, Sunshine, is settling in at the foot of the bed, or Lara has kicked her blanket off.

Since it's time for me to head up to bed anyway, I get up, then return to our third floor bedroom. We've converted the guest room behind it to the girls' room, and about a month ago we moved Anne's crib from the master to the room she shares with her sister. That's where I go now, wanting to check on the girls and the cat before climbing into bed, certain that the sooner I sleep, the sooner Damien will be beside me.

Except he's already here.

I freeze in the doorway, afraid that he's heard me. More afraid that my eyes are playing tricks on me. But it's Damien. He's sitting in the rocking chair, illuminated by the soft glow of the nightlight, his midnight black hair gleaming. He's holding

Lara in his arms, his hands cupping her sleeping head. And though he's facing the window, I can see most of him. And I know his face well enough to recognize his expression. Pain. Sadness. Maybe even desperation.

My heart hitches, and I gasp, the noise overly loud in the otherwise silent room.

I lift my fingers to my mouth, as if that will call back the sound, but it's too late. Damien looks up, and though the pain still lingers on his face, his dual-colored eyes reflect so much love and tenderness that I have to reach out for the doorframe to steady myself.

Slowly, his mouth curves into a smile that fills me up, erasing the sadness on his gorgeous features. He holds out his hand, and I go to him, craving his touch. The reassurance that all is well.

But as I walk toward my husband, this man I love with all my heart, I glimpse the lingering shadows in his eyes, and I can't shake the cold blanket of fear that settles over my shoulders when I slide my hand into Damien's.

Chapter Three

After we tuck Lara back into bed, Damien and I walk in silence to our bedroom. As soon as I close the door behind us, I expect him to speak. But he says nothing. Just sits in the armchair by the window and loosens his tie.

I go to him, then kneel at his feet, my hands on his thighs. "Damien," I whisper. "Please."

The corner of his mouth curves up. "Anything, baby. You know that."

But I don't know it. Not really. Because I've asked him to tell me what's wrong, and he's remained silent. But that's what I need. That's what will make me whole—getting into his head. Understanding him.

Most of all, helping him.

"Damien," I whisper as I look into those eyes that have seen all the way into my soul. "Please. Please tell me what's wrong."

An infinity passes between us in the space of a breath, then a small, sad smile touches his lips. "Everything is fine, Nikki. I promise."

Anger boils in me, as hot as wildfire and at least as destructive. I want to scream at him that I know something is off. I want to yell that I can practically smell the secrets. I want to beg him to tell me. Because doesn't he understand how much his silence hurts?

I say none of that, though. Instead, I press down on his thighs as I lever myself back up.

"Nikki—"

"I need to check on Anne." My voice is sharp, my words nothing more than an excuse to leave. Because if I stay, I'm going to sink to the ground and beg. But I don't want to beg. I want him to tell me. To keep his promise that there would be no more secrets between us.

In the girls' room, I peek in on Anne, sleeping peacefully in her crib with Blankie. Then I pick Kitty up from beside Lara's bed and tuck the little guy next to her. Immediately, her arm goes around her bedraggled lovey.

I close the door behind me, intending to return to the bedroom. Instead, I go outside. I pour another glass from the second bottle Jamie and I opened, then settle onto the chaise lounge and look up, letting myself get lost in the stars that blanket the moonless sky.

I don't hear him, but I know when Damien steps onto the patio. The scent of him. The subtle shift in the air, as if Damien Stark truly is the force of nature I sometimes believe him to be. Mostly, though, I am simply attuned to him, and he to me. Of course, I know he's there. Just as I knew that he would come.

I turn my head and let myself breathe him in, this man the gods must have made just for me. He's strong and powerful and walks with confidence. His strides are long and straight, and his goal is clear—me.

When he reaches my chaise, he sits on the edge of it near my hip, then takes my hand in his. I'm still wearing the bathing suit I put on to lounge with Jamie, covered by a simple, lacey pull-over. It eased up when I sat, and now Damien's slacks brush the bare skin of my thigh, making me hyperaware of our connection.

Damien lifts our joined hands, then kisses my knuckles. "Do you want to tell me what's wrong?"

My eyes dart to his, and I see both apology and humor reflected on his face. "I think that's my line," I say.

Slowly, he slips his hand beneath the lace of my cover-up so that his palm presses against the bare flesh of my lower abdomen, just above my bikini line. The touch is casual, little more than a place to rest his hand, and yet the contact sends sparks shooting down through my core, making my inner thighs tingle and my sex burn hot and needy.

I bite my lower lip and focus on my husband's face, not his touch. "Damien," I say, my voice raw with both frustration and need. "Please talk to me."

"It's work," he says. He's still holding my hand, and he releases it now to run his fingers through his hair. "Just some massive fuckery going on, and I'm trying hard not to bring that shit home."

I almost tell him that the frustration that flows off him in waves pretty much defeats his good intentions, but I stay silent. The truth is that I really do understand. Or, at least, I think I do. He's been working on an acquisition of a medical tech company for months. The deal recently went sour when the CEO turned out to be an asshole of the #metoo variety, and Damien started getting flack in the press about the fact that the deal would line the asshole's pockets.

So I understand why he's frustrated, but in the grand scheme of Stark International, walking away from one acquisition is a minor stumbling block. And that's why I think that something else went sideways with the deal. Something he's not sharing with me.

I lick my lips. "I love you so damn much," I say. "But Damien, I ..."

I draw a breath and try again. "You promised me no more secrets."

He reaches out and cups my cheek. "Baby, I know."

I swallow. Because knowing isn't the same as telling. And I'm about to say so when he draws a breath, then speaks. "Nikki, I—"

The pain in his voice is palpable, and I cover his hand on my cheek with my own. My heart pounds against my ribcage as I wait for him to tell me what troubles him.

For a moment, silence lingers. Then he says, very simply, "I just need you."

My chest tightens, and I want to scream that he can tell me. Whatever it is, doesn't he know that by now? With everything we've been through together? Everything we've shared with each other? How can he not understand?

But I say none of that. On the contrary, it's myself who gets the stern lecture. Because no matter what, I don't doubt that Damien loves me, and that's really our bottom line. Whatever it is that's going on, he's obviously not ready to tell me. I might not like it, but I can accept it. Begrudgingly, yes. But I can.

And the truth is, it's not his secret that's bothering me so much as his pain. Because I can see that he's suffering, and it hurts that he hasn't come to me for help.

Except he has.

That's why he's beside me. That's why he said that he needs me.

Tears clog my throat as I process that simple reality. "You have me, Damien. No matter what. You know that, right?"

"I do," he says. "And I'm thankful every damn day. Because God knows I don't deserve what we have."

"Yes," I say. "You do." I let go of him, then stand up. "We both do," I say as I lift the cover-up over my head, then let it fall to the deck. I reach back and untie my bikini top where it fastens at my back and neck. It pools near my feet as I watch Damien's eyes and the knowing heat that is building there.

Then I take my hand and slip it into my suit bottom, touching myself as he watches, his head cocked a little to the side, his expression hungry. "Don't make me do this alone," I tease.

"Then take them off," he says, and I comply eagerly, using my thumbs to help me wriggle out until I'm naked on the patio, my body singing with awareness and desire.

"Jamie's here?"

"She's down for the count," I say. "We polished off a lot of wine, and she and Ryan were up all last night. It's just us."

"Good." He stands, still in his suit, the tie loosely knotted around his neck. He doesn't make a move to undress. Instead, he looks me slowly up and down, his gaze hot and possessive. I can see the bulge of his erection against his tailored Savile Row slacks, and the anticipation of what's to come makes my core clench with need.

"Damien," I whisper, simply for the pleasure of his name on my lips.

His mouth curves into a grin, erasing the lingering shadows from his face. And the knowledge that I did that sends a fresh rush of desire through me. I feel the tightening in my breasts, the hardening of my nipples. My pulse pounds between my legs, and my clit begs for attention.

"Yes, Ms. Fairchild?"

I can barely conjure my voice. "You say you need me. Tell me how."

"So many ways, my love." He takes a step toward me, then dips his gaze back down to the chaise as he pulls his tie out of his collar. "But right now, I need you on your back."

I lift a brow, then look pointedly at his erection. "You

wouldn't rather have me on my knees?"

"Do I have to spank that pretty little ass?" His tone is stern. "On your back, baby. Arms above your head. Legs spread wide."

His words dance over me, making me tremble, and I comply eagerly. I straddle the chaise so that my legs hang over the sides, my toes on the flagstones. I lie back, the cushion covers cool against my bare back.

"Arms up," he says, as if I'd forgotten. "And your wrists crossed."

I do as he says, and he stands beside me holding the tie. Then he bends over me and expertly weaves it around my wrists, binding them together. Next, he loops the loose end to the frame of the chaise, then knots it, effectively binding me in place.

Out of reflex, I tug on the bond, testing its strength, but I'm not going anywhere. "Damien," I murmur as he moves to the foot of the chaise, then starts to take off his belt.

I assume that he's undressing, too, but I'm wrong about that. On the contrary, he's using his belt to bind one of my legs to the chaise, threading it through the frame, and then tightening it around my thigh. "For me to tie you at the ankle, you'd have to bring your legs together a bit," he explains. "And I like you spread open for me."

My mouth goes dry, but that's the only part of me that does. Because I can't deny that I like it too. I'm so wide, my legs are practically in splits. I had to get that way so that I could straddle the chaise. Now I'm completely exposed. And I'm incredibly wet.

Since there's nothing left to restrain me with, I assume he's going to order me to keep the other leg in place, but instead he reaches down, then rises with my bikini top, which he efficiently uses to bind me to the frame.

Now I'm exposed and helpless, and from the slow smile crossing Damien's still-haunted face, I can tell that's just the way he wants me. It's the way I want me, too. Anything to chase away those demons. Anything he needs, any time he needs it.

He knows that, of course. Knows that I'm his. Fully. Completely. Every minute of every day. And he is mine, too.

Which is why I don't understand why he hasn't confided in me. But it's also why I'm confident that he will when he's ready.

And, to be honest, I'm rapidly starting to not give a damn, because now I'm too preoccupied with the light touch of his fingertips along my calf as he trails slowly upward, his touch so light it could be the wind.

Higher and higher, his fingers dance along my inner thigh, skimming around and over the deep, angry scars that I used to be so ashamed of, but now rarely think about. Not with Damien. With Damien, I just want more, and now I whimper because he's coming so close, intentionally driving me crazy, and doing a damn good job of it.

"Damien." There's a plea in my voice, and I hear his low, smug chuckle.

"Trouble, Ms. Fairchild?"

"Please," I beg. "Touch me."

"I am touching you," he says as his fingers trail up the V of my pubic bone, then slowly stroke my lower abdomen and my pubis, never dipping lower despite the fact that my hips are rising and falling in a silent, desperate plea.

"I like that," he says. "That you want it. That you're ready. Tell me, baby. What do you want?"

"You," I say. "Always you."

"Tell me," he orders, his fingertip tracing the line of my C-section scar.

"Your fingers inside me," I say as those same fingers graze higher, teasing a pattern just below my breasts. "Your cock," I whisper. "All of you."

"Patience, sweetheart."

But I'm not patient. I'm hot and I'm needy, my skin prickling with desire, my sex clenching in silent demand, my nipples tight, and my breasts heavy.

"You're so fucking beautiful." I hear the awe in his voice and it humbles me. Then his fingers pinch my breasts, and I arch up as hot threads shoot through my body, connecting my breasts to my sex, and oh, dear God, I just *want*.

Damien.

I think I say his name out loud, but soon realize I didn't. He knows, though, and as I writhe against my bonds—wanting the friction against my skin, needing to release some of the pressure building inside me—he bends close so that his lips hover over mine, so that we're sharing breath, and then he whispers, "Do you want me to kiss you?"

"Yes. Oh, yes."

I see the smile bloom behind the heat in his eyes. "Then I will."

I close my eyes, anticipating the feel of his lips on mine. But that's not what I get. Instead, he moves between my legs, then slowly dances kisses up my inner thigh before drawing the tip of his tongue along the soft skin between my thigh and my sex. I moan, lost in the sensation of Damien's lips, his tongue, his breath.

His hands slide up my body as he laves my sex. First caressing the curve of my waist, then easing higher, his large hands spread over me, then cup my breasts, his fingers finding my nipples right as his mouth finds my clit. And then he's tugging and sucking, and sparks shoot along my body, cutting a path from my breast to my core.

I squirm, wanting more. Wanting escape. Because it's too much. The intensity. The pleasure bordering on pain, and just when I think I can't survive another second, he flicks the tip of his tongue over my clit one more time, and the world explodes around me.

I cry out, twisting and turning in my bonds, trying to bring my thighs together, to shake off Damien's hand that now cups me, but I can't. *I can't.*

And all I can do is ride the wave, gasping, all the way to the stars and back.

When the world finally settles again, I'm limp. A thin layer of sweat covers me, and I'm tingling in the cool night air.

"Holy hell," I say. "Damien. That was … wow."

"I'm glad you enjoyed it." There's truth in his voice, but a tease in his tone. "So did I. Very much."

I believe him. He wears such a self-satisfied expression, how could I not?

"Your turn," I say, dragging my teeth over my lower lip. "Untie me. Or better yet, strip and straddle my face."

His brows rise. "Why, Ms. Fairchild. How very bold."

"I want your cock in my mouth. I want to take you to the edge, but not over. And then I want you to slide down my body and fuck me so hard we both see stars."

He sits on the edge of the chaise, then leans forward and starts to untie my wrists. "Tempting," he says. "But this night was about you." He slides his hand down and cups my breast, tweaking my nipple just to the point of pain, and I moan from the pleasure of it. "I'll definitely take a raincheck, though."

He finishes untying me, then goes to the trunk where we keep towels and pulls out an oversized beach blanket. He spoons behind me on the chaise, my naked body against his fully-clothed one, then pulls the blanket over us.

"Sleep now," he says, reaching over me to check the baby

monitor on the side table, then resting his hand lightly on my sex. "Sleep. And let me hold you."

Because I'm warm and satisfied and in Damien's arms, I stop protesting and let the lull of his voice and the warmth of his body surround me, assuring me that we're back, if we were ever lost. That there is no barrier between us, no gap at all.

I fall asleep, knowing that we're fine. That, secrets or not, all is well in our world.

But when I wake to the sun, I'm all alone on the chaise, with no Damien beside me. And once again, I fear that the shadows I've seen lurking in his eyes have drawn him away from me.

Chapter Four

I check my phone, and am shocked to see that it's already past seven. Not only that, but the volume is up high and the monitor app is on. And yet neither girl woke me up.

Damien.

That explains why he isn't in my arms. He must have gotten up to feed the kids.

With a sigh, I sit up, letting the blanket fall away as I enjoy the feel of the crisp morning air on my bare skin. That's one of my favorite things about this house. That I can lie here perfectly naked and not worry about anyone seeing me. Well, no one except Damien and Jamie, and neither of them are a problem. And while the kids are still little and tucked away in their rooms, they're no hindrance either.

As for Bree…

Well, I adore her as a nanny, but it is nice when she's away.

Of course, as much as I enjoy waking up like this, it's not the caress of the morning air that I want, but Damien. Even after last night—or maybe *especially* after last night—I crave more. For that matter, with Damien, I always crave more.

My bikini top is still twisted in the leg of the chaise, and my bottoms seem to be missing. Since the lace cover-up is sheer—essentially defeating that whole covering up thing—I leave it on the chaise and wrap the blanket around me. I haven't heard a peep from Lara or Anne, but since Lara's in a toddler bed now and sometimes wanders, I don't want to take a chance on her stumbling across a naked mommy on the search for Daddy.

It's not hard to find the man in question. I hear the shower running when I enter our bedroom, and I drop the blanket onto the floor then cross the steam-filled room to the shower. I open the door and step in, sighing with pleasure when the scalding water hits my sensitive skin. Damien turns to face me, and I release a low moan, mesmerized by the sight of this man. His chiseled, perfect body, now slick with soap and steam. The hard planes of his chest. The tight muscles of his legs. And that gorgeous cock, so hard and ready it makes my mouth water.

"Looks like you're happy to see me," I say.

"I'll be happier if you grab the soap and put it to good use."

"I can do better than that," I assure him. And then I drop to my knees and do what I wanted to do last night. I bend forward and tease the tip of his cock with my tongue as shockwaves of pleasure ricochet through me from nothing more than his low, sensual groan.

I put one hand on his hip to steady myself, and with the other I stroke him. Gentle caresses building to long, teasing pulls. And my lips just barely hovering at the tip of his cock as Damien twines his fingers in my hair, his other hand pressed against the slick tile wall for balance.

He urges my head forward, but I resist. This time, he has to wait. Because right now, I want to make him as crazy—and as satisfied—as he made me last night. And I'm not going to take him in my mouth until I know that he's teetering on the brink of madness.

It doesn't take long. There's nothing about Damien's body that's a mystery to me, nor mine to him. I know how long and how hard to stroke him, taking him right to the brink. And when he's close—when neither he nor I can stand it anymore—I take his cock into my mouth. He tastes like soap and salt and musk, and the feel and scent of him send a fresh tremor coursing through me, my sex aching for him. I clench my thighs together, and even in the shower, I can feel how slick I am. I take my hand from his hip and slide my fingers between my legs. When I do, Damien tightens his grip on my hair as my head bobs, sucking and licking and teasing the length of him.

"Nikki." My name is little more than a groan, but I know what he wants, and I willingly give it to him. My surrender. My submission. I stop moving and wait for Damien to drive this show.

He doesn't hesitate. With one hand holding me steady, he thrusts forward, fucking my mouth, and I surrender to him, knowing that's what he wants. To claim me. To use me, knowing full well that I want it too. Wildly. Desperately.

The water pounds down on us, and his cock thrusts against the back of my throat. I can feel the tension in his muscles and hear his low sounds of rising passion. The knowledge that he's close resonates through me. I feel strong. Feminine.

And when he explodes in my mouth with a deep, guttural groan, I feel one more thing. I feel powerful.

He spreads his arms, leaning forward over me so that his hands on the wall are supporting his weight. Then he eases his hips back, his still-erect cock pulling free of my mouth.

Without speaking, he reaches down, pulls me up, and kisses me. It's long and deep. A kiss that starts slowly, then builds into a kiss so much like fucking, that I feel almost as if I'm still on my knees taking him in.

When we finally break apart, I'm breathless, and he's grinning. "By the way, good morning."

I laugh. "It's definitely starting out that way. And last night wasn't too shabby either."

He reaches over and turns off the water. "Definitely not."

He starts to reach for the shower door, but I take his hand, twining our fingers together. "Damien," I say. "I'm sorry about before."

"Before?"

"I know I've been pressuring you to talk about whatever's on your mind, and I'm sorry about that. We said no secrets, but maybe that's not fair. Being married doesn't mean we have to be entirely in each other's heads."

"Nikki—"

"No. That's all I wanted to say. That, and to tell you not to dress for work today."

He cocks a brow. "Somehow I don't think that naked is going to catch on as the hot new business attire."

I step back and make a show of looking him up and down. A former professional tennis player, Damien has never let himself go slack. He's tall and lean and was clearly sculpted by the gods on a particularly good day. He's also mine, and I'm not the kind of girl who shares.

"No," I say. "You're right. Not making that bold fashion statement. What I mean," I add over his chuckle, "is that I have plans for you today. Jeans will do nicely. Khakis if you prefer."

"Plans?" His voice rises with both amusement and interest.

"Yup." I grin, exceedingly pleased with myself. "Rachel cleared your schedule, and Jamie's here to watch the kids. Edward will be here in a few hours, so we can have breakfast with the girls before getting out the door. And I've already packed our bags."

"Why, Ms. Fairchild. Are you handling me?"

"You've been taking care of me for years. Now it's my turn." I move back into his arms, then tilt my face up so that his eyes meet mine. "You've been too stressed lately. I intend to make sure that for the next three days, you are very, very relaxed."

"Is that so?" He brushes a gentle kiss over my lips as his arms tighten around my waist. "I think I could get used to this."

"Good," I say, melting against him. "Because I like taking care of my husband."

"So where are we going?"

"If you treat me well enough, I just might tell you on the way." I ease back, trailing my fingers over his cock as I step toward the shower door, his low moan of frustration and longing making me smile.

"I thought I treated you pretty well last night."

"You definitely did, Mr. Stark. But just so you know, I'm a very greedy woman."

Chapter Five

"Choca-pipcakes, Daddy! Make me choca-pipcakes!"

Beside me at the kitchen table, Jamie laughs as we both watch Lara tug on Damien's khakis. She's perfectly capable of saying pancake now, but she's been calling them that since she first started talking, and neither Damien nor I want to put a stop to the cuteness.

"I'll take a choca-pipcake, too," Jamie says, grinning. "Sounds amazing, Lara."

Across the kitchen, Lara flashes a wide smile, her face already smeared from the chocolate chips that she begged from her softie of a father.

"Aunt Jamie!" Lara cries, then bursts across the room and leaps into Jamie's lap.

"Already, I'm second best," Damien grumbles.

"Well, we know who counts around here, I guess," Jamie says, holding Lara's waist as my little monkey leans backward over Jamie's legs, her fingers dangling toward the floor.

"Hey, at least you rank," I tell Damien. "Apparently I'm not even on the list."

"Mommies always have the first spot," he says to me, then walks over, spatula in hand, and kisses me sweetly, but thoroughly.

"You're cruel, you know," Jamie tells Damien. "First, you send my husband to the other side of the globe. Then you force me to watch public displays of affection."

Ryan is the Security Chief for Stark International and Damien's best friend.

"I'm pretty sure you're not starved for affection," I tell Jamie as soon as Damien's lips leave mine. "And as for the PDA, that's the price you pay for our friendship," I add, my voice high and lilting with humor.

"It's a steep price," Jamie grumbles before bending over to blow raspberries on Lara's now-exposed tummy.

"First one's ready," Damien says. "Lara, why don't you take it to your sister?"

Lara claps, and across the room, Anne joins in. "Pip-ca!" she says, then bangs on a frying pan with a wooden spoon. It's annoying, but she loves it. And for all I know, we have a burgeoning rock star in the family.

"Pip-ca!" Anne says, this time with more force.

"Annnnie. You be good!" Lara's got her stern voice on, and I watch as Jamie cracks up, then points to me. "Good impression," she says, and I roll my eyes.

At the counter, Lara carefully takes the plate from Damien, then oh-so-carefully tiptoes to the activity area we've set up in the far corner of the kitchen. It's outlined by interlocking plastic blocks and filled with every toy imaginable. Most of the time, Anne joins us at her booster seat, but the table's crowded enough this morning.

As Lara takes care of her little sister, Damien starts bringing the plates of pancakes to the table. He's made choca-pip, blueberry, banana, and plain. Which is far more than we need, but Damien never does anything by half.

"I'll keep an eye on Anne," Damien tells Lara. "Come get your pancakes."

She squeals and scurries over as I make her a plate, then pass her the syrup. She dives in, and in no time flat is a sticky little mess.

"And that's your problem," I say to Jamie as I glance at the clock. "I need to go get ready."

Damien frowns in my direction. "I thought you said we were ready. I was even under strict orders not to pack anything since you've taken care of it all."

"I have. I just have one minor wardrobe tweak to take care of. And I've got just enough time to do that before Edward pulls the limo around."

"And you're still not telling me where we're going."

"Nope." I walk to him, my arm going around his neck as I press close. "But feel free to try to persuade me otherwise," I whisper. "Feel free to try very, very hard."

He chuckles. "I'll take that under advisement," he assures me, then seals the deal with a long, slow kiss that leaves me breathless…and all the more certain that my wardrobe adjustment will prove to be very, very welcome.

"Get a room," Jamie calls from the table, making Damien and me break apart, laughing.

"The bags are by the stairs," I tell Damien. "Will you take them down while I finish up?"

"At your service," he says, the heat in his voice making me swoon.

I head for the bedroom, and the last thing I hear before disappearing inside is Damien telling Lara that he needs a goodbye kiss from his girls.

I sigh happily, thinking how lucky I am. Yes, this trip is all about eradicating the demons that have been taunting Damien lately, but even that bit of torment is only a blip compared to the incredible life I have with him and our kids and our friends. I'm ridiculously blessed, and I know it. And when I look back at the hell that was my life before LA, I'm all the more grateful for Damien and the way he's filled and colored my life.

And this weekend, I think as I strip off my clothes and step into my closet, I intend to show him just how grateful I am.

Chapter Six

Damien steps out of the limo, his attention on the smallest plane hangared at the Santa Monica airfield—his personal, customized Lear 45.

"I'm guessing we're not going to Europe," Damien says. "Canada? Mexico?"

"You're getting nothing out of me," I tease, waving to Grayson, Damien's favorite pilot.

The older man grins and rubs his graying beard as he hurries toward us. "She's good to go, Mrs. Stark. We can take off as soon as you two are on board." He hesitates for a moment, then nods to Damien, looking amused. Clearly the fact that I'm the one in charge of this particular excursion has tickled his funny bone.

"Is that all of your luggage?" he adds, glancing at the two suitcases that Edward has pulled from the limo's trunk.

"That's it," I say happily. "This is a weekend without work."

"Well, good for both of you." He signals to a lanky teen, who hurries over and takes a suitcase in each hand, easily hefting the weight. "My grandson, Gary," he says to me. "Just started working here for the summer. Saving money for college."

"That's great," I say as we follow Gary toward the plane, then walk up the integrated stairs to the crew area. From the factory, the jet's interior is set up like a luxurious commercial plane, with leather bucket seats on either side of an aisle. Unlike a commercial plane, the crew isn't locked away, but sits beyond a partition.

Because Damien likes his privacy, he made certain modifications. The cockpit is open to the flight attendant's area, but not to the passenger area. Now, the two sections are separated by a polished wooden panel and an accordion-style door.

The passenger section still boasts the leather upholstery, but now there are two oversized leather armchairs, a table large enough to either eat or work at paired with two chairs, and a plush sofa.

There's no bedroom like there is on Damien's larger planes, but I figure we'll make do. Especially since Damien's first rule for the flight staff is that if the Do Not Disturb light is on, no one enters the passenger area except in a life-threatening emergency.

It's a rule I approve of. Especially today. I have plans for Damien, after all.

I've asked the crew not to announce our flying time or destination. So once we're airborne, I'm the only one who knows how much time we have before landing. Honestly, it's kind of nice. There aren't many occasions where Damien Stark doesn't have all the relevant details right at his fingertips.

He laughs when I tell him as much. "I think I'm man enough to trust my wife to get us wherever we're going."

"Oh, it's not just the destination," I say. "It's the ride."

We'd buckled in side by side on the sofa, but now that we've reached cruising altitude, I stand and go to the wet bar, then pour him a double shot of Booker's bourbon over ice. I walk slowly back to him, then stand in front of him, my legs spread. I've already kicked off my ballet flats, and I'm wearing a loose pullover dress in a soft jersey material. It's short-sleeved and hits mid-thigh, and all Damien would have to do is reach for the hem and lift it slightly to get a very intimate view of what's underneath. Which, frankly, isn't much.

So little in fact, that just standing this way—my legs spread, the air caressing my sex, my mind imagining what's to come— has me wet and ready. A fact that I'm sure Damien realizes, because I'm essentially braless, and my now-hard nipples are hard to miss under the clingy material.

His eyes lock on mine. "Something on your mind, Mrs. Stark?"

"Just that this trip is all about you. And I have something for you."

"I'm intrigued."

"I like you that way," I say, then grab the hem of the dress, tug it over my head, and toss it aside, all in one motion.

I try to watch Damien's face, and I see his eyes widen in surprise and pleasure at what I've revealed. Specifically, me. All wrapped up in a pretty red bow. One life-size present for him to play with.

"Christ, Nikki. I don't know if I should frame you or fuck you."

"The latter, please. There's something very erotic about dressing this way."

"There's something erotic about seeing you that way."

I've taken a Christmas bow and used double-sided fashion tape to position it low on my pubis, hiding my pussy from view. And as for my breasts, well, that required some doing— and Jamie's help—but we managed to essentially concoct a cup-less bra by wrapping red ribbon over and under my breasts in a criss-cross pattern, then tying it off in the back.

The real kicker? I'm wearing nipple jewelry. Clamps that look like rings for pierced nipples, but are really just attached using pressure. Which started out uncomfortable but has progressed to rather fabulous.

And both of the rings have tiny stars dangling from them. With the stars and the ribbon, I look like something that should be under the tree.

"You look like something that should be in my lap," Damien counters when I tell him my tree theory. And about that, I wholeheartedly agree.

"I think, Mr. Stark, that if you want to be fucked senseless on this ride, you need to unfasten those slacks."

He starts to, then halts his hands, deliberately puts them on the arm rests, and says, "I think you should do that." And when I start to bend over to free his cock, he adds, "With your mouth. And only your mouth."

His words send tremors of lust tumbling through me, and I'm more eager than I probably should be to use my teeth to tug down a zipper. But eager I am, and so I kneel in front of him.

Before I can tilt forward to put my mouth at his fly, he reaches out, tugging lightly on one of the nipple rings. I tilt my head back as the sensation from that connection shoots right to my clit and an uncontrolled shiver, like an orgasmic Coming Attraction, unsettles me.

"Do that again and I won't have the patience to use my mouth," I say, and this time he behaves as I bend over and, with some effort, manage to get the button open and the zipper down. He takes pity on me next and helps free his cock from his briefs and slacks. Though I'm not sure how much was pity and how much was desperation. My mouth dancing on his cock through his clothes has made him grow rock hard. So hard in fact that I don't want to wait any longer.

But once again, Damien steps in first, ordering me onto the couch with him. "Straddle me," he says. "I want that pretty pussy just barely brushing the head of my cock. Make me crazy, Nikki. I want you to make me moan."

"With pleasure, Sir," I say, then do as he says, straining my thighs to adjust my height above him to the perfect distance. Thankfully, I've been working out like a fiend in the months since Anne's birth, and my muscles aren't crying out in protest yet.

The rest of me is starting to weep though. Not in pain, but in frustration. I'm teasing him, yes. But I'm teasing me, too. Light caresses to my clit. The sweet promise of penetration pulled back at the last minute.

Fire rages in my core, and I want him inside me. Deep and fast and hard.

Damien's holding me by the waist, but now he slides his hands down to cup my ass and I bite my lower lip, knowing what's coming next. And when he moans and says, "Oh, baby," I tell him to check under the blanket on the seat next to him.

He does, finding the remote control for the butt plug I'd inserted as the very last step in the day's outfit. Damien had surprised me with it before we were married, and I'd relished being at his mercy.

Now I am again as he holds the remote but doesn't activate it, leaving me tense and horny and more than a little desperate.

But that's okay. There's one part of my desperation I can satisfy right now, and as I tease his cock with my pussy, I also reach down, taking his shaft in my hand and positioning him right at my center.

"Nikki…"

"Damien, I need you to fuck me. I need you inside me." And without waiting, I lower myself onto him, so wet and so ready that he fills me completely. And just as I've settled myself and am rocking with him, my clit rubbing against him, he turns on the vibrator, making me arch back, and cry out, unable to contain the rush of wild, wicked lust that gallops through me before breaking free.

"That's it, baby. You are so fucking beautiful. Ride me, baby," he orders, and I do. My hands on his shoulders as I ride him hard.

I'm close, and I know he is too. Our bodies are matching each other. Breaths. Moans. An almost discernible tremble that courses through his body, matching the electric tingle that shoots up my thighs toward my core.

"Damien," I whimper. Because I'm close. So close. And then, "Oh, my God," I cry as the plane hits an air pocket and I'm bounced up and then pounded back down on him, a violent, tidal orgasm crashing over me as Damien explodes inside me, his own release at least as powerful as mine.

He holds me close as my body shakes and shimmies, the lingering flutters of electrical pleasure dancing over the surface of my skin.

"Best present ever," he says as he pulls me close and I curl up on his lap. I glance down, then flash a wry grin. "I think you're going to have to change those slacks," I tell him at the same time that the intercom bursts on and the attendant, Katie, apologizes for the unexpected air pocket.

I meet Damien's eyes and we both start laughing, clinging tight to each other in post-coital, hysterical bliss.

I don't know what's been bothering Damien. But in that moment at least, I know that he's put it behind him.

And as I cuddle close, naked and sated, I can only hope that his demons stay away from our weekend.

Chapter Seven

Just as I'd requested, there's a car waiting for us when we land at the Oakland airport. I make a mental note to tell Rachel that she pulled everything off perfectly.

While the driver whisks our bags to the trunk, we say goodbye to Grayson. Since it's only a long weekend, and I confirmed that the other fleet pilots can handle transportation for the Stark International execs this weekend, I told Grayson to take the weekend off and enjoy San Francisco. I even offered him a room at the hotel where Damien and I are staying. He declined, explaining that his oldest daughter lives in Silicon Valley. So as soon as he's hangared the plane, he's heading that way.

"And where are you taking me now?" Damien asks once we're ensconced in the plush backseat of the Lincoln Town Car.

"We'll drop our bags at the hotel, and then I have our itinerary all mapped out."

"Itinerary," he repeats, sounding amused.

"It's important," I say indignantly. "Maybe you've been to San Francisco before, but this is only my second trip. And on the first one, all I saw was the inside of some hotel ballroom while I went through the paces for a Miss Junior Hoopdedoo pageant."

His mouth twitches. "Not a pageant I'm familiar with. But I'm sure you blew them all away."

I scowl, because I had. And that victory when I wasn't even a teen yet had spurred my mother to push and push and push, going to any lengths in her obsession to gain me yet another tiara.

"Moving on," I say, because I am not letting my mother creep into this weekend. "I thought about staying someplace funky and unusual, but to be honest I couldn't find a place that had everything I want other than the Stark Century-Nob Hill."

"As it should be," he says, buffing his fingernails on the front of his Henley shirt that he's paired with the fresh khakis he changed into.

I aim an exaggerated eye roll his direction. "Yes, you're amazing. Your properties are amazing. Your employees are amazing."

"And my wife is amazing," he concludes, taking my hand and pressing my palm to his chest. "Which is why I always keep her right here."

"Don't make me melt," I whisper. "We're not in the limo." The Town Car is plush, but there is no privacy screen in this particular model.

"Not to worry," he says with a perfectly straight face as his free hand moves to the hem of my dress and starts to gently stroke the soft skin of my thigh. "Every Stark employee signs a nondisclosure."

"Don't even think about it," I say, even though my body clearly has other ideas. I feel the heat pooling between my legs, and if the driver looks back, he'll undoubtedly see how hard my nipples are. "Damien. Stop."

Gently, I push his hand away, and he shifts position, hooking his arm around my shoulder and tugging me close.

"You sure?" he teases. "We've never made love with someone looking. I've never claimed you like that, letting anyone who's watching know that you're mine. Only mine. *Completely* mine."

"And you never will," I say, even as a sensual shiver trills up my spine. We've watched other people make love—despite everything that went wrong, that night in Paris was incredible—but we've never been on display. And I've always said that I don't want to be.

But I can't deny that it makes for a delicious fantasy.

I meet Damien's eyes, expecting to see a teasing humor there. Instead, I see genuine heat. The kind that shoots to my core and would soak my panties if I were wearing any. Apparently, I'm not the only one with wild fantasies on my mind. And so help me, I want him so much right now that I almost lean over and claim his mouth with mine.

But Damien's kiss is magical; it steals my reason as it floods my senses. His kisses make me hungry. Not for food, but for him. And I'm too afraid that if I kiss him my resolve will be shaken, and it won't matter to me at all whether or not our driver can see everything.

Good God, what's gotten into me?

The answer, of course, is simple. *Damien.*

Resolutely, I scoot to the left, putting a good two inches between us. Beside me, Damien chuckles, the bastard. I know damn well that he understands exactly what I'm thinking.

I clear my throat. "At any rate, we're in the penthouse. I was going to simply take one of the suites, but then I looked at the online brochure, and—"

"The rooftop patio."

"Yeah," I say. "I figure the view must be amazing."

"Yes," he says, his gaze sweeping over me. "I'm sure it will be."

I sigh, delighted with not only his words and intimation,

but also with the fact that Damien still affects me as deeply now as he did when we first got together. Although no, that's not true. It's deeper now. A wildfire of new passion burns now like the interior of the sun, self-sustaining and unimaginably hot.

I force my attention back to the list on my phone. "That's where we'll have lunch—in fact, it should be waiting for us when we arrive."

"Good. I'm starving." But the hunger I see in his eyes isn't for food, and I have to laugh.

"You're insatiable."

"Where you're concerned? Absolutely."

"Good," I say firmly. "I wouldn't have it any other way."

"So after our … meal … what next?"

"We're taking the ferry to Sausalito for a late afternoon bike ride along the waterfront. Then we're taking a limo back to the hotel because, well, I tend to enjoy limo rides with my husband."

"What a coincidence. I enjoy limo rides with my wife."

"Then tomorrow we explore the city. I want to see that winding street and Fisherman's Wharf and Golden Gate Park. And sea lions. Aren't there sea lions around here?"

"If there aren't, I'll buy you some."

"Big spender," I tease. "And then in the afternoon we'll have a late lunch on the water in a private boat tour, then at sunset we'll go check out Coit Tower before grabbing dinner somewhere. I'm thinking Chinatown, but haven't decided."

"That's quite the itinerary."

I frown. "Too much?"

"There's never too much where you're concerned. And so long as you've kept room in the schedule for me to have you naked…"

I roll my eyes. "Mr. Stark, you have a one-track mind."

"Is that a problem?"

I force myself not to laugh. "Shopping for the kids needs to be on the agenda, too. But there are probably shops in Sausalito. And maybe at the Wharf?" I frown, then look back up at him sheepishly. "I know this is a romantic outing, but do you think we could call the kids when we get to the hotel?"

"Sweetheart, I think I might have to insist on it."

"Thanks." I snuggle against him. "Funny how life changes. One day you look at it a certain way, and then just a few years later you look back. And even though everything's the same, it's different, too."

"It's fuller," he says, and I nod in agreement. Because that's exactly how I feel.

He strokes my hair, and I sigh with pleasure. "Do you have any idea how much I love you?" he asks.

"I think I have a clue."

We sit like that for a moment, looking out at the view as we head over the Bay Bridge. It's peaceful. Romantic. Even sweet. And right then, I'm so glad that I arranged this. He needed it, I think. Hell, *we* needed it. Whatever ghost was haunting him at Stark International, now at least we're far, far away.

At least that's what I think until his phone chirps. I lift my head, frowning because he told me he set it to silent.

"Sorry. I wasn't expecting this. There are only four people whose calls can go through this weekend, and one of them is sitting next to me."

I'm certain that two of the others are Jamie and Rachel— this weekend's babysitter and his assistant. I have no idea who the fourth is, but if Damien is allowing the call to ring through, I'm sure it must be important. I just hope that answering it doesn't push Damien back into the dark from which I'm trying to drag him.

"Nikki?"

"I'm sorry. I didn't realize you were waiting on me. Answer it, of course."

He does, and my chest tightens when I see the relief bloom on his face as he takes the call. "Tell me," he says without preamble.

He listens, his features tightening, then relaxing slightly when he says, "Well, that's good news at least. No, go ahead and put it through. One way or the other, I need to know." He glances at me, then looks away so quickly that it feels almost like a physical shove. "As quickly as possible, but you already know that. Yeah, I understand. And thanks, Quincy. Tell Dallas I owe him one."

He clicks off, then pinches the bridge of his nose, his eyes closed as if he's fighting a headache. When he opens his eyes and looks at me, his expression is both guarded and apologetic.

"It's okay," I say, though I'm not sure it is. Not now that I see the hint of shadows that I thought we left behind blooming in his eyes. "Who is Quincy and what does he have to do with Dallas?"

Dallas Sykes is the CEO of a longstanding department store chain who earned the nickname The King of Fuck because of his reputation as a playboy heir who romanced women, spent money, and basically wasted his life. Of course, all that changed after he got married—but that was scandalous, too, as his wife happened to also be his adoptive sister, Jane.

The thing is, I've gotten to know Dallas a bit, and I'm quite certain that his reputation is manufactured. What I don't know is what's hidden under that fine-looking exterior. Damien does, I'm sure, but that's the kind of secret I don't mind him keeping. Yes, I want to know. But it's not his story to share. Even so, I'm certain that there *is* a story. Especially since Damien recruited away one of Dallas's former employees, Noah Carter, a brilliant programmer who would have been wasting his skills if he'd really only been doing work for a department store chain.

"Quincy Radcliffe. An employee of Dallas's with unique skills. I have him poking around for me. Doing a bit of investigation."

I nod, assuming this has to do with the botched acquisition, and since I want as little work creeping into this weekend as possible, I only nod and change the subject. "Any thoughts on where to go for dinner tomorrow? I suppose we can ask the concierge at the hotel. If he's a Stark employee, he's got to be knowledgeable."

"I like your idea of Chinatown," Damien says as the Town Car starts to climb the hill, approaching the hotel. "But why don't we play it by ear? I may be in the mood to have my wife for dinner."

"Cute," I say, but lean up against him, sighing happily as his arm tightens around me.

"As for today, I like your plan." He bends his head close to my ear, his voice pitched just for me. "I'll just add that after drinks on the roof this evening, I intend to make love to you until you pass out. So we might want to grab a bite before we get those drinks."

"Oh," I say, my core clenching. I lick my lips. "Well, I think that's a fine addition to our itinerary."

"And tomorrow morning, we can walk around the corner to this charming little diner I know of."

"I thought I was supposed to be taking care of you this weekend," I say.

"How about we take care of each other?"

I take his hand and squeeze it. "I can live with that."

His mouth brushes my ear. "I want you now," he murmurs. "Thank God we're almost to the hotel."

"Yes." The word is almost a moan. "Thank God for—"

But my words are cut off by the sharp *beep* of the driver's horn as he slams on the brakes.

"Sorry," he calls back. "The guy in front of me stopped short. And look at that mess. Something's going on."

He's right. There are cars parked at odd angles blocking the street in front of the hotel. I see some officers trying to get the crowd to move, and someone appears to be arguing with the hotel valet.

"I can get you a bit closer. And then I can take the car into the garage and park. I'll make sure your luggage gets right up to you, sir."

"Much appreciated." Once the driver pulls over, Damien leans forward to tip him, then reaches over me to open the door. I step out, Damien beside me, then immediately freeze as dozens of people swarm toward us, cameras clicking and microphones extended. It's a cacophony of indistinguishable voices, and I turn, reaching for Damien who stands behind me, looking even more shellshocked than I feel.

Then the noise starts to form into words, and the words slam against me with the force of a wrecking ball.

"Mr. Stark! Damien! Is it true? Did you father a child with Marianna Kingsley?"

Chapter Eight

Before I even have time to think, Damien has tugged me back into the Town Car. He yanks the door shut, smacks the back of the front seat, and urges the driver to, "Go! Just go!"

He does, and soon we're inching out through the sea of reporters and paparazzi. The windows aren't tinted, and Damien pulls me toward him, obviously with the intent of hiding my face in his chest. But I jerk away and bend over, my head in my hands and my eyes screwed tightly closed.

"Nikki…" He puts a tentative hand on my back, but I don't respond. I can't. My mind's on overload, and it's taking every ounce of my concentration to simply keep from screaming.

A child?

Damien has another child?

The words slice through my head, as cold and sharp as a steel blade. I stay hunched over, tucked into myself until the Town Car finally makes it into the valet garage. I hear the door open and a man's voice fills the car.

"Mr. Stark, I'm so sorry. I have no idea how anyone even knew you were coming. Your wife made the arrangements and we assured her complete confidentiality. I promise you, I will personally get to the bottom of this and terminate whoever is responsible for this leak."

"We'll talk," Damien says in a voice I've only rarely heard. One that contains a controlled explosion. "In the meantime, my wife and I would like to go to our room."

"Of course. I have your key right here."

"Nikki." All harshness has left his voice. It's as gentle as I've ever heard it. As gentle as it was when he found me on my floor years ago after I'd hacked off all my hair in a last ditch effort to keep myself from cutting.

I draw a breath, then look into my husband's eyes. *A child. How could he not tell me he had a child?*

"Come on out of the car," he says. "Let's go up."

One more breath. Then another. I straighten, then hold out my hand. "Give me the key," I say, my voice raw. "I need time."

I watch as his face shatters, as visibly as if I'd shoved my fist into a mirror. "Nikki." It's my name and his voice, but it's almost unrecognizable under the weight of all his pain.

A child.

Dear God, has he slept with another woman?

My stomach lurches, and I fear that I'll be sick.

No. No. A thousand times, no.

Not Damien. Not that.

But even with that certainty pounding in my head, I can't bear the thought of going with him to the room. I look away, not meeting his eyes as I slide out of the car, then hold my hand out to the manager. "I'd like to go to my room now."

The man's eyes dart over my shoulder, his expression like a scared rabbit. Damien must nod, because suddenly relief paints the man's face and his lips curve into a professional smile. "Of course. Jacob can show you up. Your luggage will be along shortly."

He signals to one of the bellmen lingering by the door, and

Jacob and I start walking toward the service elevator. I know that Damien is watching me go, willing me to turn around, to extend my hand and tell him to come with me.

But I don't.

I can't.

And so I face the wall until the elevator begins to ascend. Then I slowly turn, stare hard at the back of Jacob's neck, and will myself not to cry.

* * * *

The penthouse is amazing, just as I'd known it would be. Three walls of mostly glass and a stunning view of San Francisco. But I barely even notice.

I pace the room, my thoughts roiling with every step, and in a room this large, I can take a lot of steps.

He did this to us.

Damien.

This is all on his shoulders. All of it. The press assault. Being blindsided. The whole rotten, miserable experience.

And as for the child … well, maybe he did that to us, too. Who the hell even knows?

Except I do, of course. Or, at least, I know enough to know that he didn't have an affair. No matter what else, I know that for certain. Damien would never cheat on me. His devotion is my true north.

His name is still echoing in my thoughts when the door opens and a bellman rolls a cart in, Damien right behind him. I stiffen, then sit ramrod straight on the edge of the couch while Damien gives the guy a tip, then puts out the Do Not Disturb sign and locks the door.

When he comes back to me, I see the resolve and the apology on his face.

"I haven't touched another woman since you, Nikki," he says, and I shock us both by bursting out laughing.

I laugh so hard I actually slide off the couch and end up on the floor. So hard that my chest hurts and I have to force air into my lungs. It's hysteria, of course, but in a way it feels good. It's pain, and goddamn me, I need that now.

But I need to talk to Damien, too, and so I force myself into control, then breathe deep until I get my voice back. "Good God, Damien, do you think I don't know that?"

I push myself up off the floor so that I'm standing right in front of him, my head tilted back, my eyes locked on his, all his pain and regret reflecting right back at me. But I have no pity. Not now. Not after everything.

"You've known this was coming, haven't you? You've known that there was a bomb buried right between us. You've known for days. *Days*, Damien. And when I asked you about it, you lied."

He opens his mouth, but I lift a finger, cutting him off.

"Trouble at work? Why would you tell me that? Why wouldn't you just tell me the truth?" I taste salt and realize that tears have been streaming down my face. My vision is blurred and I wipe them away, then sigh as I sit again. "Tell me now, Damien. Tell me everything."

For a moment, he just stands there. Then he drags his fingers through his coal black hair, nods, and begins.

"I went out with Marianna a few times the year before you moved to LA. A friend introduced us. She wasn't looking for anything serious—or so she said—and it seemed like a good idea at the time."

I nod, remembering what Damien said when he first pursued me—that before me, he didn't date. He fucked.

They were careful, he said. He used a condom. She said she was on the pill. But neither method is infallible—Anne is proof of that—and so it's theoretically possible that the little boy really is Damien's.

"I've seen pictures of him," Damien admits. "Dark hair. Blue eyes. It's possible."

I nod. Damien's eyes aren't blue, but Jackson's are. And since Jackson is his half-brother, Damien could have that recessive gene, too.

In other words, based on looks alone, the little boy—Nate—could really be Damien's. "Is he?" I ask. "Is the boy yours?"

He shakes his head. "I don't know. I demanded a paternity test. She declined. Maybe that means I'm not. Or maybe it just means that her attorney isn't willing to take a chance until he has a hefty settlement from me."

"Attorney?"

Damien nods. "The bastard demanded I set up a trust for Marianna and the child or else he'd leak everything to the press." His mouth twists wryly. "I wasn't expecting it quite this soon."

"And Charles?" I ask, referring to Damien's attorney.

"I've talked to him. He advised me not to petition the court for a paternity test since that would surely end up in the press. Like I said, we weren't expecting this. Not now."

"Well, what were you expecting?" I snap.

"To handle it." His voice is pretty snappy, too. "To get the whole goddamn mess resolved."

"And what? Then I wouldn't even have to know about it?"

"Christ, Nikki. You know me better than that."

"Do I? Because honestly, I'm not sure. I mean, you didn't tell me any of this."

"No," he says simply. "I didn't. I couldn't."

"Why not?"

He hesitates, opens his mouth, then closes it again. Then he shakes his head and drags his fingers through his already-mussed hair. "I don't know."

The answer is like a stab through my heart. "I see." I push myself to my feet. "I need some time," I say, then start to head for the door.

I feel lost. Vulnerable. But when Damien reaches for me, I shake him off, which only makes fresh tears prick in my eyes. Because Damien is my rock; he's the one I go to when I'm vulnerable. Only now he's turned our world upside down.

"Nikki—"

"No. I need some space. I just—I just need to be alone right now."

I don't wait for him to answer. I don't take a key or grab my purse. And I don't turn around to look at him. If I do, I know I'll start crying again, and I can't do that. I need space. I need to pull myself together and figure out what to do. Except there isn't anything *to* do. The situation is what it is.

But it's not the situation that's twisted me up in knots. It's the way Damien handled it. The way he kept me out of it. The way he put up a wall of lies. Or at least obfuscations.

That's between us now, and the weight of that reality has knocked my entire world off kilter.

I barely even notice riding the elevator to the lobby. And it's not until I'm sitting at the bar that I realize I even had a destination in mind. It's almost one now—we should be heading for Sausalito, but so much for that plan—and as far as I'm concerned it's well past time for a drink.

I order a bourbon on the rocks with a cherry, then amend that to make it a double. It's my lunch, after all. But when the bartender brings it, I don't take a sip. Instead, I use the tiny straw to stir the drink, watching the ice move, the motion relaxing. Almost hypnotic.

"You look like a woman who's had a hard day. And it's

really far too early in the day for that."

I look up to find myself staring into a pair of gorgeous gray eyes. The man's not too bad either. He's tall and trim and looks like he just came from a fashion shoot for a corporate catalog.

"I'd buy you another," he says in the wake of my silence. "But you haven't touched that one yet."

"No. But thank you for the offer." I'm about to tell him that not only do I want to be alone, but that I'm married. Which he must know, since the engagement ring I wear next to my wedding band is winking under the bar's lighting.

But I don't have to say anything to the man at all. Instead, a familiar voice behind me says a single word. "Leave."

Gray Eyes looks over my head at Damien. For a moment, I think he's going to argue. Then he holds up his hands and takes a step back. "Just chatting with the lady."

"The lady is mine."

Since I still haven't turned to look at Damien, I'm not surprised when Gray Eyes looks at me, his expression like a question mark. I nod, he glances from me to Damien, then he inclines his head, turns, and saunters out of the bar.

One beat, then another. I know Damien is still behind me; I can feel him there, as if his presence alone reshapes the fabric of reality.

After a moment, I can't stand it anymore. "If you're staying, at least come around here where I can see you."

He does, taking the stool beside me and signaling that he'll have what I'm having.

I take a sip, and when his drink arrives, he does the same. A moment later, he says, "I'm so sorry, Nikki," and once again I have to blink back those damn tears.

"You say you couldn't tell me. But, Damien, this is us. Do you know what those words did to my heart?"

"Do you know what it did to mine seeing that boy's face?

Realizing that he looks like me? Christ, Nikki. The thought of having a child that I didn't know about. A child who isn't yours. Ours. A baby I never saw grow or heard speak a first word. You know what that means to me."

He curses softly, then lifts his glass and downs the whole damn thing. Then he turns and looks at me. "How do I tell the woman I love—the mother to my little girls—that if that boy is mine, I have to be in his life. I *have* to be."

His words reach out and twist my heart, and I have to will myself not to cry again. Of course, he would have to be in Nate's life. Damien would never be absent. Would never hurt a child by his absence, or any other way. He knows too well what it means not to have a real father. Just as I know what it means not to have a real mother.

I reach over and take his hand, and the instant I touch him I know that we'll get through this. God knows we've been through worse.

"Damien," I say softly. "I get it. But all you had to do was tell me. Did you really think I wouldn't understand?"

"Yes. No." He releases a frustrated sigh. "Hell, Nikki, I…"

I wait for him to finish, then swallow when he says nothing else and that gulf between us increases again. "I know you weren't celibate before me. It's not the fact of this child that bothers me. That's not what hurts. What hurts is that you built a wall, Damien. Brick by brick, you've been building a wall between us these last few days. And I never in a million years would have believed that could happen."

He rubs his temples. "I know."

I take a long sip of my bourbon, then push it away from me. "I'm going back to the room. Are you coming?"

"In a minute," he says, reaching for the rest of my drink.

I give him a tight nod, then extend my hand. "Do you have a key?"

He passes it to me, and it all seems so normal that I can hardly get my head around it. I start to reach for him, then pull my hand back, unsure if he even wants my touch right now.

The thought breaks me a little more, and I turn away, then hurry out of the bar, both relieved and disappointed when I step on the elevator and see that Damien really hasn't followed me.

As the doors close, I lean my head against the wall, trying to remember when I'd felt this helpless. Not since Germany. Not since Damien was on trial for murder and pushed me away, thinking he'd save me by freeing me. But it hadn't worked. And this time he's not pushing me away, not really. We're exactly the same distance apart as we were before. But there's that goddamn wall between us now.

Fuck.

I left my phone in the suite when I went down to the bar, and I return to find it ringing. I hurry to the living area and glance down at the coffee table where I left it, expecting that the call is from Damien, but it's not. It's from Jamie. And she's called at least twice.

Dear God, the kids.

I snatch the phone up and press the button to answer the call. "What's going on? Are the girls okay?"

"The girls?" Jamie's voice rises with incredulity. "Are *you* okay?"

For the first time, it hits me that this whole mess is out there for all the world to see. And isn't that just too fucking special?

"No," I say honestly. "I'm not okay."

"Didn't figure you were. How's Damien?"

I don't tell her that he's the reason I'm not okay, not the existence of a little boy named Nate. I should tell her. She's my best friend. And if I can't go to Damien, then it's Jamie that I want to cling to.

Except right now, I just want to sleep. I don't care that it's not even dinner time or that I had such carefully made plans for the day. None of that matters now. I just want to close my eyes, forget it all, and hope that the sun shines brighter tomorrow.

And the only real comfort I can take is the surprising, unexpected realization that even though everything feels like it's going to hell, I haven't once thought of taking a blade to my skin.

Chapter Nine

I went to sleep expecting to wake in Damien's arms, because even when we argue, we both find solace in the other's touch.

But when I'm awakened by the morning sun streaming in through the windows, I realize that I'm alone. Frowning, I roll over, looking at Damien's side of the bed. The covers are rumpled, but I don't know that he's slept there. I tossed and turned all night. The twisted bedding is probably from me. Especially since his side of the bed is cool to the touch.

Which means I slept alone. And so did Damien.

I choke back a sob, then lay back down, pulling my knees up to my chest. All I want is to go back to sleep. But I know I can't. Damien and I are both ripped up, I know that. But I also know that the only way we'll heal is together.

I have to buck up and find him.

That's not as easy as it should be. The penthouse is huge, but I search every room, and there's no Damien. That's when I remember the rooftop patio. I head out to the balcony, then climb the stairs, relief flooding me when I see him standing beside one of the support columns for the rooftop cabana.

I start to walk toward him, but pause when I see that he's not alone. There's another man with him, my view of him no longer blocked by the cabana. A lean man, ruggedly handsome, with deep set eyes and a hard expression.

And, apparently, very good hearing, because the moment I gasp in surprise, he turns those eyes to me. Automatically, I smooth the dress I've been wearing since yesterday. At least I didn't come up here in my robe. Or naked.

I take a step toward them, my eyes on Damien and not this stranger, a man with a primal, dangerous air about him. "I didn't realize we had company," I say, and though I'm trying hard to keep the reprobation out of my voice, I'm sure a hint of it comes through.

"I didn't want to wake you."

"I told him this wouldn't take long," the man says, his voice surprisingly sensual, all the more so because of its deep British accent. "I'm Quincy."

"Oh!"

"Quincy Radcliffe," Damien says. "My wife, Nikki." He extends a hand to me, and I go to him gratefully, not realizing until I slide my hand into his how deeply I needed to feel the touch of his skin against mine.

"I apologize for the intrusion, but my investigation led me to San Francisco anyway, and I thought I would tell Damien the good news in person."

"Good news?" I echo. "Good news would be great."

They both smile at that, and we settle around the table that doubles as a fire pit.

"I told you on the phone that I was able to obtain a DNA sample from the child," Quincy says to Damien. He's about to continue, but I hold up my hand.

"Wait. What?" I look to Damien. "Can we back up?"

Damien turns to me. "I told you that Marianna and her attorney—"

"Boyfriend," Quincy interrupts. "He is an attorney, but he's her latest man, too. The woman's a gold digger, no doubt about it. You, my friend, were one of many. And frankly the top of the heap. She's been sliding down ever since. The current one's something of a git. And the bloke she was with six months ago had actor on his resume, but you'll only find him on the porn sites."

"I won't be looking," Damien assures him, and under the circumstances, his cavalier comment makes me smile. Damien's a man who needs action. And now that he's told me the truth and things are happening with Quincy, maybe the shadows will fade.

"At any rate," Damien begins again, "I told you that Marianna and her boyfriend demanded that I make arrangements for the child, but refused my request for a paternity test. Marianna cried and Warren—the boyfriend— spewed some bullshit about how with my resources I could totally buy off the lab. That she hadn't slept with anyone else in the relevant time, and that if I didn't pony up, then they'd take her story public."

"And you didn't want to file a lawsuit because the publicity from that would take you to the same place they were threatening."

"Exactly." He glances at Quincy. "So I took matters into my own hands, and that's how Quincy ended up here. He got his hands on a DNA sample of the kid. And he's working to track down the real father."

"Not working," Quincy says. "Done. I found him last night. Daniel Bryson. That's the main reason I came here today," he adds. "Otherwise, I wouldn't have interrupted your weekend."

"Hang on," I say. "Let's back up. Like, who are you? I thought you worked for Dallas."

I watch as Quincy shoots Damien a questioning look, and Damien shakes his head just slightly.

I exhale. "Dallas doesn't really run his family's department store, does he?"

"Actually, he does," Quincy says. "But I don't work there. Though I do work for Dallas."

I turn my attention to Damien, since Quincy is being cryptic.

"Let's just say that there's a lot more to Dallas than meets the eye. And part of what's under the surface is a very well-funded group of investigators and, well, agents."

"He means mercenaries," Quincy says. "Some would say vigilantes. Though it's as well that we don't say so. I'm with MI6 officially. Unofficially, I moonlight at Deliverance."

My eyes widen. "Oh. I see." Not the whole picture, I'm sure, but at least the high points. Because I've heard of Deliverance. Quincy's right—it's considered a vigilante group. And it's responsible for finding, rescuing, and returning dozens of kidnapping and human trafficking victims.

I meet Damien's eyes. "There *is* more to Dallas than people know. But I can't say I'm surprised, having met him a couple of times." After a moment, I frown. "But what aren't you telling me? Because this is just a paternity question, isn't it? If you were only trying to track down the kid's DNA, do you really need MI6? I mean, can't Ryan's staff handle it?"

"If Ryan were available, he could have handled it personally," Damien agrees. "But this isn't something I want leaked within the company. I trust my people, but I don't like shining a secret into someone's face and then forcing them to keep it. Better to go out of house."

"So you called Dallas."

"And he called me," Quincy said. "I did a bit of hustling and managed to get a clean DNA sample after a day of tailing the kid. Soda can. Third try and we got a specimen. And you, my friend, are in the clear. As far as you, me, and the Stark

Medical Labs are concerned, Specimen-N and Specimen-D are in no way related."

"Thank you," I say, even as Damien says the exact same thing. He glances at me and smiles, then takes my hand.

"Too bad they went public already," Quincy says. "I'm not sure why they did. Once the cat was out of the bag, they couldn't hold the promise of silence over your head."

"To shame me, I assume. But I've been in more unpleasant positions with the media. I'll have my PR team issue a press release with the private paternity test results and my sincere hope that Ms. Kingsley can find her son's father." He takes my hand. "And that will be the end of that."

"Except that the poor kid is living with that woman," I say. "You're *not* the father, which means that the line about you being the only possible guy was bullshit. The whole thing was a scam. Hell, she might have even slept with you as part of a long con. And that poor little boy has to grow up with that creature."

"Maybe not," Quincy says. "I told you, I believe I may have found the real father."

"How the hell did you manage that?"

Quincy shrugs. "Lots of footwork. And I may have inappropriately used government resources to check her cell phone records during the period about nine months before the kid's birthday. It stood to reason that if she was shagging him, she was probably talking to him as well. One would hope, anyway."

"And the guy?" Damien asks.

"He lives in Oakland. He's a school teacher. Seems to be a solid chap. Apparently he was an investment broker when Marianna latched onto him. I assume she believed that he'd go far. Dumped him the day after he told her he wanted more out of life than sitting in an office chasing numbers."

"But what about the boy?" I ask.

"He wants to be part of the boy's life. Assuming he is the father. I submitted his lab work this morning."

I reach for Damien's hand. "So Damien's clear, and we're just waiting to see if this guy really is the father? And how Nate fares?"

"And for the Stark publicity machine to begin churning to clear his name. Nasty ambush of you two last night, I'd say."

"I'd agree," Damien said. He extends his right hand, holding tight to me with his left. "Thank you."

"My pleasure. I'm sure we'll work together again someday. But for now, I'm heading to South Hampton before popping back over to London."

"And do you have a wife or children, Mr. Radcliffe?"

"Quincy. Or Quince if you prefer. And no," he says with a hard edge to his voice, "there is no Mrs. Radcliffe."

"I'll walk you down," Damien says. "Do you want to order breakfast?" he asks me.

"Of course," I say. "Goodbye, Quincy. And thank you."

He takes my hand, kissing it instead of shaking. I watch them go, and I can't help but think that this man has at least as many secrets as Damien does. And if that's the case, then God help him.

Damien's back in less than the time it takes me to order breakfast, and he steps behind me as I'm finishing the call, hooking his arms around my waist and pulling me in close to him, then nibbling on my ear as I try to finalize our order.

"Stop," I say once I'm off the call.

"Why stop now? You're finished."

I spin in his arms. "You're better. I'm glad."

I watch the play of emotion over his face. Then he takes a step back, his fingers twined with mine. He leads me to the chairs that overlook the city, and when he sits in one, he pulls me into his lap along with him.

"I don't know if this is going to make sense or not," he begins, "but until all this started, I thought that I knew fear."

I shift, my brow furrowing as I try to understand.

"Before, I mean. The times when I thought I would lose you. Sofia. My trial. I thought it would all come apart. That you'd be ripped from me."

He shifts to look me straight in the eyes. "But that wasn't fear. Fear is knowing that there are two tiny, precious people in the world that I'm responsible for. It's looking at them and wondering if they're going to be screwed up because I'm screwed up. It's knowing that they depend on me. And I'm so goddamn afraid that I won't be the man for them—for you—that you want and need me to be."

I blinked away tears and nod. "I know. Damien, of course I know. Did you think I couldn't understand that? If not me, then who?"

He just shakes his head. "I thought it was going to be me. That boy's father. The hair. The blue eyes. Hell, even the shape of his chin. And I thought about going to you. Telling you that I had a son—"

"You don't," I say, sliding my fingers into his hair. "But if you did, it would be okay. We'd figure out a way to have him in our life."

He's still for a moment, then he pulls me close and buries his face in my breasts before pushing me back and claiming my mouth, hard and fast, with so much passion it melts me.

"Well, hello to you, too," I say when he breaks the kiss.

"Christ, I love you. And I—ever since we brought Lara home, I've been—oh, hell. I didn't think I could love you more. But I did. And we have a family. A *family*. And it feels perfect. And you know how much of a miracle that is to me. To both of us."

I nod. I definitely understand that.

"I was afraid I'd fucked it up for good."

"Never," I say, moved by his vulnerability and by the force of his love. "You couldn't possibly."

This time when he kisses me, it's slow and sweet. I sigh deeply and pull back, wanting to see the face of the man who is my whole life.

"Make love to me, Damien," I say. "I want to get lost in your arms. I want to fly."

"As you wish, Mrs. Stark," he says, then proceeds to take me to the stars.

Chapter Ten

I watch as Damien paces in front of the patio railing, all of San Francisco spread out beyond him, the Golden Gate Bridge gleaming in the morning light. His hands are in his pockets, and his expression is unreadable.

I wish I could hear the full conversation, but the only pieces I get come when Damien says something into the headset hooked over his right ear. And so far, Charles Maynard, his attorney on the other end of the line, has been doing most of the talking.

"All right, then, I think we're good to go. Call me if you have any trouble with McGregor, and email me if it all goes smooth. But I don't expect trouble." He laughs. "Exactly. That's why I hired you after all. You're the most bad ass shark in all the water."

He chuckles again, says goodbye, then tugs off his earpiece and tosses it onto the chair. "And that's the end of that. Or, I hope it is."

"The most bad ass shark?"

"He's a lawyer. And he'll get the job done."

"You're really not worried?" I ask, and Damien shakes his head.

"It should be smooth sailing. With the results of the

paternity test, they'd be fools to move forward or to slander me publicly. Marianna may not have resources, but with a well-placed lawsuit, I could bury her attorney."

"That's McGregor, right?"

He nods. "And if they don't call off their hounds and retract the statement by noon, Charles is going to be all over them like a shark on chum."

"Because he's the baddest of them all."

"In the legal world, being bad is being good," he says with a grin.

"So I guess it's really over. For us, anyway. I still feel bad for that poor kid."

"That's *not* over," Damien reminds me. "Not until we know for sure that Bryson's the father. And then not until he decides what to do."

"What if he's not the father? Or what if he decides to just walk away? That boy. With that mother." The thought makes me shudder.

"From what I know of Marianna, and from what Quincy's said, she was along for the ride, and this whole scheme was manufactured by McGregor. It's not the first time he's primed the pump for a bullshit settlement. There've been a lot of ethical violations filed. Some slaps on the wrist, but he's never been disbarred."

"So Marianna is just out for a rich husband? She's not a manipulative bitch?" I make a face. "It's better for the kid. But not *better.*"

"I know, baby. But there's only so much we can do. And we shouldn't do anything until we hear about Bryson."

I nod, then inspect my cuticles, uncertain how Damien's going to take my next off-beat comment. "Fair enough. But either way, maybe the Stark Education Foundation could keep an eye on him. And if it looks like he needs it, maybe an anonymous grant could get floated the kid's way?"

Gently, Damien tilts my chin up. "And that's why we are what we are to each other," he says softly. "Because we think alike."

* * * *

The call from Quincy comes through when we're out on the bay. Damien's not an expert sailor, but he's an advanced amateur, and since we wanted privacy, we rented our own boat instead of taking a chartered tour of the bay.

We've been on the water for about an hour, and now we're anchored so that we can sit down to the picnic lunch we brought with us, the basket put together by the Stark Century Hotel kitchen.

"So tell me good news," Damien says in lieu of a greeting when he answers the phone. This time it's on speaker, so I can hear both sides.

"I have plenty to tell." Quincy's cultured voice is sharp and crisp. "Mr. Bryson is the father. I had the lab expedite the tests, and there's no legitimate question."

"That's great news," I say. "At least, it's great if Bryson wants to be involved in the boy's life."

"He does indeed. So much that he's started the ball rolling. He's already preparing a petition asking the court to establish custody, and his attorney assures him his chances are great. He said to thank you for recommending Charles Maynard's firm. He was surprised at how low the hourly fee is."

I look at Damien, who shrugs as I rise up onto my knees, lean over, and kiss him.

"You're a good man, Damien Stark," I say once the call has ended. "I'm so lucky that you're mine." And I'm so happy that the world has shifted back to normal.

With a sigh, I scoot closer, settling in between Damien's legs as he puts his arms around me. Our plan was to spend the entire day on the boat, have champagne at sunset and make love in the fading light, then fly home tonight so that we're there tomorrow to have breakfast with the girls.

But now…

"Damien?" I twist in his arms so that I can see his face. "Would you do something for me?"

"You know I would, baby. Anything you want. Anything you need."

"Could we go home now? I know we haven't really gotten to enjoy San Francisco, but it's not going anywhere. And honestly, I really want to see the girls."

"Yeah," he says with a tender smile. "I think that's a great idea." He bends and kisses my forehead. "Anything else?"

I consider the question, but then shake my head as I smile back at him. "You've already given me everything, Damien. Right now, all I want is for you to kiss me."

And as the boat bobs on the waves, I melt into my husband's embrace and lose myself in the sweet sensuality of his touch, his kiss, his everything, enjoying these last moments together before we're on our way back to our house, our girls, our *home*.

* * * *

Also from 1001 Dark Nights and J. Kenner, discover Damien, Indulge Me, Hold Me, Tame Me, Tempt Me, Justify Me, Caress of Darkness, and Caress of Pleasure.

Sign up for the 1001 Dark Nights Newsletter
and be entered to win a Tiffany Key necklace.

There's a contest every month!

Go to www.1001DarkNights.com to subscribe.

As a bonus, all subscribers will receive a free copy of
Discovery Bundle Three
Featuring stories by
Sidney Bristol, Darcy Burke, T. Gephart
Stacey Kennedy, Adriana Locke
JB Salsbury, and Erika Wilde

Discover 1001 Dark Nights Collection Five

Go to www.1001DarkNights.com for more information.

BLAZE ERUPTING by Rebecca Zanetti
Scorpius Syndrome/A Brigade Novella

ROUGH RIDE by Kristen Ashley
A Chaos Novella

HAWKYN by Larissa Ione
A Demonica Underworld Novella

RIDE DIRTY by Laura Kaye
A Raven Riders Novella

ROME'S CHANCE by Joanna Wylde
A Reapers MC Novella

THE MARRIAGE ARRANGEMENT by Jennifer Probst
A Marriage to a Billionaire Novella

SURRENDER by Elisabeth Naughton
A House of Sin Novella

INKED NIGHT by Carrie Ann Ryan
A Montgomery Ink Novella

ENVY by Rachel Van Dyken
An Eagle Elite Novella

PROTECTED by Lexi Blake
A Masters and Mercenaries Novella

THE PRINCE by Jennifer L. Armentrout
A Wicked Novella

PLEASE ME by J. Kenner
A Stark Ever After Novella

WOUND TIGHT by Lorelei James
A Rough Riders/Blacktop Cowboys Novella®

STRONG by Kylie Scott
A Stage Dive Novella

DRAGON NIGHT by Donna Grant
A Dark Kings Novella

TEMPTING BROOKE by Kristen Proby
A Big Sky Novella

HAUNTED BE THE HOLIDAYS by Heather Graham
A Krewe of Hunters Novella

CONTROL by K. Bromberg
An Everyday Heroes Novella

HUNKY HEARTBREAKER by Kendall Ryan
A Whiskey Kisses Novella

THE DARKEST CAPTIVE by Gena Showalter
A Lords of the Underworld Novella

Discover 1001 Dark Nights Collection One

Go to www.1001DarkNights.com for more information.

FOREVER WICKED by Shayla Black
CRIMSON TWILIGHT by Heather Graham
CAPTURED IN SURRENDER by Liliana Hart
SILENT BITE: A SCANGUARDS WEDDING by Tina Folsom
DUNGEON GAMES by Lexi Blake
AZAGOTH by Larissa Ione
NEED YOU NOW by Lisa Renee Jones
SHOW ME, BABY by Cherise Sinclair
ROPED IN by Lorelei James
TEMPTED BY MIDNIGHT by Lara Adrian
THE FLAME by Christopher Rice
CARESS OF DARKNESS by Julie Kenner

Also from 1001 Dark Nights

TAME ME by J. Kenner

Discover 1001 Dark Nights Collection Two

Go to www.1001DarkNights.com for more information.

WICKED WOLF by Carrie Ann Ryan
WHEN IRISH EYES ARE HAUNTING by Heather Graham
EASY WITH YOU by Kristen Proby
MASTER OF FREEDOM by Cherise Sinclair
CARESS OF PLEASURE by Julie Kenner
ADORED by Lexi Blake
HADES by Larissa Ione
RAVAGED by Elisabeth Naughton
DREAM OF YOU by Jennifer L. Armentrout
STRIPPED DOWN by Lorelei James
RAGE/KILLIAN by Alexandra Ivy/Laura Wright
DRAGON KING by Donna Grant
PURE WICKED by Shayla Black
HARD AS STEEL by Laura Kaye
STROKE OF MIDNIGHT by Lara Adrian
ALL HALLOWS EVE by Heather Graham
KISS THE FLAME by Christopher Rice
DARING HER LOVE by Melissa Foster
TEASED by Rebecca Zanetti
THE PROMISE OF SURRENDER by Liliana Hart

Also from 1001 Dark Nights

THE SURRENDER GATE By Christopher Rice
SERVICING THE TARGET By Cherise Sinclair

Discover 1001 Dark Nights Collection Three

Go to www.1001DarkNights.com for more information.

HIDDEN INK by Carrie Ann Ryan
BLOOD ON THE BAYOU by Heather Graham
SEARCHING FOR MINE by Jennifer Probst
DANCE OF DESIRE by Christopher Rice
ROUGH RHYTHM by Tessa Bailey
DEVOTED by Lexi Blake
Z by Larissa Ione
FALLING UNDER YOU by Laurelin Paige
EASY FOR KEEPS by Kristen Proby
UNCHAINED by Elisabeth Naughton
HARD TO SERVE by Laura Kaye
DRAGON FEVER by Donna Grant
KAYDEN/SIMON by Alexandra Ivy/Laura Wright
STRUNG UP by Lorelei James
MIDNIGHT UNTAMED by Lara Adrian
TRICKED by Rebecca Zanetti
DIRTY WICKED by Shayla Black
THE ONLY ONE by Lauren Blakely
SWEET SURRENDER by Liliana Hart

Discover 1001 Dark Nights Collection Four

Go to www.1001DarkNights.com for more information.

ROCK CHICK REAWAKENING by Kristen Ashley
ADORING INK by Carrie Ann Ryan
SWEET RIVALRY by K. Bromberg
SHADE'S LADY by Joanna Wylde
RAZR by Larissa Ione
ARRANGED by Lexi Blake
TANGLED by Rebecca Zanetti
HOLD ME by J. Kenner
SOMEHOW, SOME WAY by Jennifer Probst
TOO CLOSE TO CALL by Tessa Bailey
HUNTED by Elisabeth Naughton
EYES ON YOU by Laura Kaye
BLADE by Alexandra Ivy/Laura Wright
DRAGON BURN by Donna Grant
TRIPPED OUT by Lorelei James
STUD FINDER by Lauren Blakely
MIDNIGHT UNLEASHED by Lara Adrian
HALLOW BE THE HAUNT by Heather Graham
DIRTY FILTHY FIX by Laurelin Paige
THE BED MATE by Kendall Ryan
PRINCE ROMAN by CD Reiss
NO RESERVATIONS by Kristen Proby
DAWN OF SURRENDER by Liliana Hart

Also from 1001 Dark Nights

TEMPT ME by J. Kenner

About J. Kenner

J. Kenner (aka Julie Kenner) is the *New York Times, USA Today, Publishers Weekly, Wall Street Journal* and #1 International bestselling author of over one-hundred novels, novellas and short stories in a variety of genres.

JK has been praised by *Publishers Weekly* as an author with a "flair for dialogue and eccentric characterizations" and by *RT Bookclub* for having "cornered the market on sinfully attractive, dominant antiheroes and the women who swoon for them." A six-time finalist for Romance Writers of America's prestigious RITA award, JK took home the first RITA trophy awarded in the category of erotic romance in 2014 for her novel, *Claim Me* (book 2 of her Stark Trilogy) and in 2018 for her novel Wicked Dirty (Wicked Nights, Stark World).

In her previous career as an attorney, JK worked as a lawyer in Southern California and Texas. She currently lives in Central Texas, with her husband, two daughters, and two rather spastic cats.

Visit JK online at www.jkenner.com
Subscribe to JK's Newsletter
Text JKenner to 21000 to subscribe to JK's text alerts

Lost With Me
The Stark Saga Book 5
By J. Kenner
Coming October 23, 2018

From New York Times and #1 International bestselling author J. Kenner comes a new full-length novel in the wildly popular Stark Saga that's left millions of readers breathless.

His touch takes my breath away. Our passion feeds my soul...

My love for Damien fills me, and the intensity of our bond brings me to my knees. For him, there is no burden I wouldn't bear, no decadent punishment to which I won't submit.

The dark days seemingly behind us, we have carved a life out of adversity, chiseling away pain to reveal strength and beauty. Now, all I want is to laugh with our children in the sunlight, then surrender myself to Damien's embrace in the dark.

But lingering secrets and hidden menace threaten our family. Now, Damien and I must forge a new strength from our shared passion and hope the fire between will burn away the darkness and protect everything we hold most dear.

This sexy, emotionally charged romance continues the story of Damien Stark, the powerful billionaire who's never had to take "no" for an answer, and his beloved wife Nikki Fairchild Stark.

Damien: A Stark Novel
By J. Kenner
Coming January 8, 2019

From New York Times and USA Today bestselling author J. Kenner comes a new story in her Stark series...

I am Damien Stark. From the outside, I have a perfect life. A billionaire with a beautiful family. But if you could see inside my head, you'd know I'm as f-ed up as a person can be. Now more than ever.

I'm driven, relentless, and successful, but all of that means nothing without my wife and daughters. They're my entire world, and I failed them. Now I can barely look at them without drowning in an abyss of self-recrimination.

Only one thing keeps me sane—losing myself in my wife's silken caresses where I can pour all my pain into the one thing I know I can give her. Pleasure.

But the threats against my family are real, and I won't let anything happen to them ever again. I'll do whatever it takes to keep them safe—pay any price, embrace any darkness. They are mine.

I am Damien Stark. Do you want to see inside my head? Careful what you wish for.

Indulge Me: A Stark Ever After Novella
By J. Kenner
Coming July 9, 2019

Despite everything I have suffered, I never truly understood darkness until my family was in danger. Those desperate hours came close to breaking both Damien and me, but together we found the strength to survive and hold our family together.

Even so, my wounds are deep, and wispy shadows still linger. But Damien is my rock. My hero against the dark and violence.

And when dark memories threaten to consume me, he whisks me away, knowing that in order to conquer my fears he must take control. Demand my submission. Claim me completely. Because if I am going to find my center again, I must hold tight to Damien and draw deep from the wellspring of our shared passion.

Discover More J. Kenner/Julie Kenner

Tame Me: A Stark International Novella by J. Kenner
Now Available

Aspiring actress Jamie Archer is on the run. From herself. From her wild child ways. From the screwed up life that she left behind in Los Angeles. And, most of all, from Ryan Hunter—the first man who has the potential to break through her defenses to see the dark fears and secrets she hides.

Stark International Security Chief Ryan Hunter knows only one thing for sure—he wants Jamie. Wants to hold her, make love to her, possess her, and claim her. Wants to do whatever it takes to make her his.

But after one night of bliss, Jamie bolts. And now it's up to Ryan to not only bring her back, but to convince her that she's running away from the best thing that ever happened to her--him.

* * * *

Tempt Me: A Stark International Novella by J. Kenner
Now Available

Sometimes passion has a price…

When sexy Stark Security Chief Ryan Hunter whisks his girlfriend Jamie Archer away for a passionate, romance-filled weekend so he can finally pop the question, he's certain that the answer will be an enthusiastic yes. So when Jamie tries to avoid the conversation, hiding her fears of commitment and change under a blanket of wild sensuality and decadent playtime in bed, Ryan is more determined than ever to convince Jamie that they belong together.

Knowing there's no halfway with this woman, Ryan gives her an ultimatum – marry him or walk away. Now Jamie is forced to face her deepest insecurities or risk destroying the best thing in her life. And it will take all of her strength, and all of Ryan's love, to keep her right where she belongs…

* * * *

Hold Me: A Stark Ever After Novella by Julie Kenner
Now Available

My life with Damien has never been fuller. Every day is a miracle, and every night I lose myself in the oasis of his arms.

But there are new challenges, too. Our families. Our careers. And new responsibilities that test us with unrelenting, unexpected trials.

I know we will survive—we have to. Because I cannot live without Damien by my side. But sometimes the darkness seems overwhelming, and I am terrified that the day will come when Damien cannot bring the light. And I will have to find the strength inside myself to find my way back into his arms.

* * * *

Justify Me: A Stark International/Masters and Mercenaries Novella by J. Kenner

McKay-Taggart operative Riley Blade has no intention of

returning to Los Angeles after his brief stint as a consultant on mega-star Lyle Tarpin's latest action flick. Not even for Natasha Black, Tarpin's sexy personal assistant who'd gotten under his skin. Why would he, when Tasha made it absolutely clear that—attraction or not—she wasn't interested in a fling, much less a relationship.

But when Riley learns that someone is stalking her, he races to her side. Determined to not only protect her, but to convince her that—no matter what has hurt her in the past—he's not only going to fight for her, he's going to win her heart. Forever.

* * * *

Caress of Darkness: A Dark Pleasures Novella by Julie Kenner
Now Available

From the first moment I saw him, I knew that Rainer Engel was like no other man. Dangerously sexy and darkly mysterious, he both enticed me and terrified me.

I wanted to run—to fight against the heat that was building between us—but there was nowhere to go. I needed his help as much as I needed his touch. And so help me, I knew that I would do anything he asked in order to have both.

But even as our passion burned hot, the secrets in Raine's past reached out to destroy us ... and we would both have to make the greatest sacrifice to find a love that would last forever.

Don't miss the next novellas in the Dark Pleasures series!

Find Me in Darkness, Find Me in Pleasure, Find Me in Passion, Caress of Pleasure...

* * * *

Storm, Texas.

Where passion runs hot, desire runs deep, and secrets have the power to destroy...

Nestled among rolling hills and painted with vibrant wildflowers, the bucolic town of Storm, Texas, seems like nothing short of perfection.

But there are secrets beneath the facade. Dark secrets. Powerful secrets. The kind that can destroy lives and tear families apart. The kind that can cut through a town like a tempest, leaving jealousy and destruction in its wake, along with shattered hopes and broken dreams. All it takes is one little thing to shatter that polish.

Rising Storm is a series conceived by Julie Kenner and Dee Davis to read like an on-going drama. Set in a small Texas town, Rising Storm is full of scandal, deceit, romance, passion, and secrets. Lots of secrets.

On behalf of 1001 Dark Nights,

Liz Berry and M.J. Rose would like to thank ~

Steve Berry
Doug Scofield
Kim Guidroz
Jillian Stein
InkSlinger PR
Dan Slater
Asha Hossain
Chris Graham
Fedora Chen
Kasi Alexander
Jessica Johns
Dylan Stockton
Richard Blake
and Simon Lipskar

Made in the USA
Middletown, DE
27 August 2018